Dedalus Euro Shorts
General Editor: Timothy Lane

CLEOPATRA
GOES TO
PRISON

Claudia Durastanti

CLEOPATRA GOES TO PRISON

translated by Christine Donougher

Dedalus

Published in the UK by Dedalus Limited
24-26, St Judith's Lane, Sawtry, Cambs, PE28 5XE
email: info@dedalusbooks.com
www.dedalusbooks.com

ISBN printed book 978 1 910213 96 4
ISBN ebook 978 1 912868 42 1

Dedalus is distributed in the USA by SCB Distributors
15608 South New Century Drive, Gardena, CA 90248
email: info@scbdistributors.com   web: www.scbdistributors.com

Dedalus is distributed in Australia by Peribo Pty Ltd
58, Beaumont Road, Mount Kuring-gai, N.S.W. 2080
email: info@peribo.com

First published by Dedalus in 2020
Cleopatra va in prigione copyright © Claudia Durastanti & Minimum Fax 2016
Published in agreement with the MalaTesta Lit Ag.Milano
Translation copyright © Christine Donougher 2020

The right of Claudia Duarastanti to be identified as the author of this work has been asserted by her in accordance with the Copyright, Designs and Patents Act, 1988.

Printed and bound in Great Britain by Clays Elcograf S.p.A
Typeset by Marie Lane

This book is sold subject to the condition that it shall not, by way of trade or otherwise, be lent, resold, hired out or otherwise circulated without the publisher's prior consent in any form of binding or cover other than that in which it is published and without a similar condition including this condition being imposed on the subsequent purchaser.

THE AUTHOR

Claudia Durastanti is a writer and literary translator based in London. Her critically acclaimed debut novel *Un giorno verrò a lanciare sassi alla tua finestra* won the Premio Mondello Giovani in 2010. She is the author of four novels. *Cleopatra goes to Prison* is her first novel to be translated into English.

Claudia is one of the rising stars of Italian fiction.

THE TRANSLATOR

Christine Donougher was born in England in 1954. She read English at Cambridge University and after a career in publishing is now a freelance translator of French and Italian. Her translation of *The Book of Nights* by Sylvie Germain won the 1992 Scott Moncrieff Translation Prize.

Christine has translated *Senso (and other stories)* by Camillo Boito, *Sparrow (and other stories)* by Giovanni Verga and *Cleopatra goes to Prison* by Claudia Durastanti, for Dedalus from Italian.

Her translations of *The Price of Dreams* by Margherita Giacobino and *Venice Noir* by Isabella Panfido from Italian will be published by Dedalus in 2020.

1

Every Thursday Caterina visits her boyfriend in prison.

Visiting hours are from two to three in the afternoon: usually she takes a bus and walks some of the way to the detention centre, which is signposted – not that she has ever got lost in Rebibbia.

For Caterina the prison smell is that of the flaking iron gates and the aftershave of the clerks who sit beneath calendars with pictures of German Shepherd dogs on them, so she overdoes it with the perfume, hoping Aurelio can get a whiff of it across the space separating them during her visits.

Actually, she also writes short letters to him that arrive at the prison a couple of days later; she sprays the sheets of paper with perfume until they are almost transparent and plasters them with kisses the way she did with photos of the singers she liked when she was in middle school.

Aurelio says his cellmates take the mickey, but if he doesn't get the letters he is disappointed.

CLEOPATRA GOES TO PRISON

Rebibbia is overcrowded, Caterina can tell from the noise, like that of a junior school canteen. Aurelio has described his room to her – he never calls it a cell – and the guys he shares it with, three drug dealers who speak a consonant-heavy language and consider themselves professionals because they're not drug users.

At first they cooked together, then Aurelio offered to do it for all of them and his mother began sending him various brands of tinned food. The empty cans are supposed to be confiscated straight after the meals but the inmates use them as ashtrays: in prison everything is metallic, even boredom.

Having checked in, Caterina takes a seat in the area reserved for family visits: Aurelio gives a wan smile as soon as he sees her.

To get to visit her boyfriend she had to have a special interview with the prison governor, a kindly overweight man who explained to her his reluctance to make an exception to the rules.

"It would be unfair to all the other girls in your position, who aren't spouses, I don't make any exceptions, not even for the foreigners or the ones with no family."

It was late afternoon and the governor had apologised for having no lights on in his office, artificial illumination gave him a migraine. Caterina had nodded, continuing to stare at the photo of the President of the Republic hanging behind the desk: the sunspots all over his cheeks and skull made him look as if he were already dead.

"I am an exception: you don't know how many years I've been coming here," she had replied with a smile.

"Did you have long to wait in line?" asks her boyfriend,

collapsing on to the chair.

Caterina shakes her head – Aurelio has stopped thinning his eyebrows, it makes him look more casual, handsome.

"Your lips are cracked, I must remember to bring you a lip salve."

"There's no point, I'm always biting them."

During the visit they talk about how their mothers are, she only gets cross when Aurelio apologises for having ended up in prison.

"Nice lipstick."

"Someone lent it to me, it's called Russian Red."

"And I've got a perfume called Black Opium. Doesn't that make you laugh?" she persists when he remains silent.

"It sounds like a 007 movie... show me your hands."

Caterina unclenches her hands and spreads her fingers. Her fingertips are peeling, the cleaning chemicals make them blister and go red. Her fingernails, which at one time she used to paint with designs that could win the admiration of the girls behind the bar, are short and suffering from calcium deficiency.

Aurelio was arrested during an operation to clean up areas in Rome known for drug-dealing and prostitution; he and his business partner, Mario, were running a nightclub where, according to the prosecution, the dancers rendered services not included in the price list.

When the place was closed down Caterina was left without a job and now works as a receptionist in a hotel in the heart of Tiburtina.

"You said they didn't make you do any cleaning."

"Staff shortage."

She changed the subject to avoid his clingy sadness.

"Down at the garage someone brought in a Fiat 600 – shades of the past."

"Are they still around?"

Caterina's father used to run one of the most respected car repair shops in Pietralata and during a period of expansion he took on two full-time mechanics.

"No one knows why but mechanics are always brothers," he explained to her the day he hired them: Caterina was eight years old and helped him with the job interviews.

She liked those two men because they turned up wearing blue overalls and sunglasses as if they were supposed to be taking part in a Grand Prix. They had taken over the workshop when her father went back to live in Abruzzo but they left the name unchanged as a mark of respect.

She still drops by sometimes and it amuses them to leave black smudges on her cheeks.

"Your father was mad, he had you driving when you were this small," they told her recently, indicating knee height for the benefit of a client who wanted only to know what they were going to charge him. "He held you in his arms and let you take the steering wheel."

Caterina remembered, it was one of the few times her father had frightened her.

Whenever anyone left him with an expensive car – he never had a Porsche, but there had been a lot of saloon cars – he would tell her to get in, then activate the autolift until the car was just below the ceiling and she would be left suspended there to play with the buttons and controls on the dashboard, pretending to be in a spaceship.

She had gone everywhere in that workshop, travelled

beyond Jupiter and colonised Mars, taken Barbie to the Moon and seen fireworks created by the blowtorch.

"He had a finely tuned ear for the engine," the mechanics would say eagerly, smiling, then embarrassment would always set in because their thoughts would turn to where the former owner was now, to the talent he could no longer use. After his arrest for the grooming of a minor, the repair shop motto had become: *"Anyone can make a mistake."*

At the age of nineteen Aurelio had a sky-blue Fiat 600, a grown-up Topolino.

They used to listen to electronic music in it, and Caterina liked to go for a spin on the orbital that was closed to traffic after midnight. They would drive along the stretch that swept past a particular row of apartment buildings near Largo Preneste almost going right through their windows, while dust, caught in the street lights, showed up on the dashboard, along with reflections of the green and copper-coloured buildings. A gleam produced by the abrasion of the sky against the flypaper-like strips of cement made her happy.

Then Aurelio passed the Fiat on to his brother, who was ashamed to be seen driving round in it, and the virginity that had been lost on those seats meant nothing to him.

"I've started working out again."

"It shows," says Caterina, even though it's not true.

"I do press-ups against the wall like a Buddhist."

She laughs. "Imagine if you were to become religious while you're in here. How do you know what Buddhists do?"

"I got a book out of the library. You know what Raoul said to me when I moaned about not being able to use a punchbag? 'Use me,' he said. The guy's crazy."

Caterina thinks of the times when she lay on her back and whispered the same thing to him, when they were kids and their bones and nerves had hardly finished developing, and being in bed meant trying out whatever their bodies had just discovered they were capable of.

At a certain point during the visit Aurelio asks her who could have framed him.

"Listen, I was thinking last night…"

"You should get some sleep," Caterina says, touching the dark circles under her eyes. "Otherwise you'll end up like this."

"That has nothing to do with sleep, you were born with your eyes like that. It occurred to me last night, it must have been one of the girls, someone who had it in for Mario."

"Do you need any money? Your mother said she can send you some more."

Aurelio pulls a face. "You never want to talk about it."

"They're things you have to ask him about," she replies. But Aurelio's friend and ex-business partner is in Venezuela and doesn't send postcards.

"I don't need any money," he says, ruffling his thick clean hair.

Caterina thinks of him taking a shower, would like to ask if it's different from taking a shower with his mates at the gym, but is afraid of the possible suggestiveness in her voice.

Aurelio puts his lips to the palm of his hand.

"That's what I miss," he says, baring his teeth, and she gives a groan.

"Me too." Caterina draws closer, grateful not to have to touch his thin chest.

Aurelio had always been slight and the skin could be pulled away from his bones like old tissue paper dug out of the lockers for school holiday decorations, paler than watercolours in a flea market.

The kickboxing competitions he used to take part in had toughened him up but after six months in prison he once again looked like the cocky impoverished kid who had been waiting for her outside school, standing with his arms folded in front of a Fiat 600. He told her she could drive it if she wanted to, but first he complained he had never seen her laugh.

Caterina waves a hand, by way of bemoaning the lack of air; prison is a micro weather station incapable of mitigating the external temperature – in summer you melt, in winter your breath freezes into shards.

"Actually, tell my mother to send me a hundred euros if she can."

"Your brother's graduating on the fifteenth, I thought of buying him a watch. What do you think of this one?" she says, pulling out a newspaper cutting showing a pilot watch.

"I don't like the colour, but go ahead. As long as it doesn't cost too much."

"Leave it to me, I'll sign the card from both of us."

"A brother who's an engineer," says Aurelio, shaking his head.

"You never want to talk about it," she teases him.

"God knows who he takes after."

Aurelio stares at the mould in the corners of the room and feels ashamed, the paint on the walls is a lung that does not breathe and does not work.

"I can't work out who framed me," he says, continuing to

stare at the wall.

"No one framed you, Aurelio, you got yourself into trouble."

"Don't call me by my name. It sounds cold-hearted. I may not have a degree but it doesn't take a genius to realise someone ratted to the police."

"And what difference would it make knowing who?"

Before opening the nightclub he and his friend had run a video rental store in Torpignattara; it was doing well, then they couldn't pay the taxes they owed to the State as well as those demanded by the local racketeers. They told everyone the digital revolution was to blame but Caterina knew they said that because they were embarrassed they had not been able to fend for themselves.

"I have to go," she says, to cauterise the conversation.

Aurelio blows her a kiss and before getting to his feet, adds: "I saw the same watch on the guy who arrested me."

When she gets her identity card back at the security checkout Caterina remembers the time a prison association organised an open day for families and she brought Aurelio's nephew to the playground.

While the child was being pushed on the swing by his uncle, she stood chatting with one of his cellmates. They talked about the star-shaped tattoos behind his ear and in the crook of his arm; until then she had only ever seen ones like that on girls.

"It was something that didn't work out. I want to get a constellation done, but I don't know whether I've got enough skin left," said the inmate. Caterina thought she was being nice to him but when they were saying goodbye he burst out,

"You're getting out, anyway," in an abrupt, wounded tone, and she was ashamed at having thought, "I deserve it."

On the way back she glimpses the mauvish mountain peaks; they are ethereal and distant like figures behind a smokescreen.

Caterina stops off in the parking lot behind an electrical appliances shop, running her fingers through her hair, which is wet from the slight drizzle, and a man inside an unmarked police car hoots his horn. He always picks her up after her prison visits because they don't have much time to see each other and using public transport would make the situation even worse.

When she gets in the car the policeman kisses her, ruffling her hair which she has just tidied. He asks how Aurelio is doing.

"Same as ever. He seems less depressed, talks rubbish about the future," she replies, pulling out the newspaper cutting to check whether the watch she wants to buy Aurelio's brother is the same as the one on his wrist.

The policeman starts the engine and she asks if his shift the night before was long and dangerous.

"Not especially, we took a schizophrenic woman to the Pertini hospital after complaints from neighbours who heard her quarrelling with her mother for stealing her medication. She collapsed in the car, but at A & E they prioritised a woman who had drunk a glass of orange squash and I had to argue with the nurses to get her admitted."

"Orange squash sends you to A & E?"

"Her son had dissolved his methadone in it because he didn't like the taste of the methadone on its own."

"Is she still alive?"

"She is, the schizophrenic isn't: insulin shock."

Caterina nods with a bitter taste in her mouth.

"You're quiet today," says the policeman, checking on his hair in the rear-view mirror.

"It's Aurelio. I don't know what to do about him." Caterina squints against the light reflecting off the dashboard, her new contact lenses dehydrate her eyes.

"You don't have to do anything," he says, stroking her bare leg – she always wears a short skirt when she goes to the prison even if Aurelio can't see anything from where he is seated.

"He keeps wondering who it was, he doesn't understand it was a random inspection you carried out."

"If you attract a certain type of clientele, people talk. Try and tell him that next time." The policeman parks close to a cast-iron cannon dedicated to the war dead – this is the first time he has brought her to his place.

He does not like living in this area but his salary does not yet allow him to move to a residential neighbourhood; his grandfather left him the apartment and he has done no more than repaint it.

Thanks to his working hours, he does not have to spend too much time among these low square-roofed houses, where the plastic awnings the neighbours have put over their front doors look like faded strips of red liquorice, and Sunday morning lie-ins are disturbed by the rumble of the carwash in his apartment building.

"I've never told you anything, I've never helped anyone with their inquiries," says Caterina, walking beside him.

Before crossing the road she points to a supermarket covered with stickers and Chinese characters. "Aurelio and Mario had a video rental store right there."

"That's funny, last month we found a girl walled up alive on the floor above. Dodgy massages, money laundering, I'm not allowed to talk about it."

Caterina turns to see if he is joking, but the policeman is staring at the pavement.

"However, you did tell me something about the nightclub world. Your boyfriend is surrounded by talkers," he says, taking her by the arm – he is not as yet capable of holding her hand when they are out for a walk. At the crossing, she stops at the traffic lights, the smell of petrol fumes makes her gorge rise.

"That's not true, don't say it even as a joke. I can't bear it, I've never told you anything."

"What flavour ice cream do you want?" asks the policeman as they cross, and Caterina replies that on Thursdays she is never hungry.

In the late afternoon they make love in the bath; the policeman sucks her steam-softened wrists and Caterina's blood runs hot and frantic like the ink spilled from smashed Bic biros. "I can't believe you've never done it before. You're thirty," he says to her, before lying her on her stomach. When he lifts her pelvis Caterina smiles and replies, "I'm a dancer not an animal."

Later, as they drink water in the living room under the ceiling spotlights, she gets the ammoniac aftertaste of betrayal – which is what prevents her from sleeping and makes her eyes red and watery, like a rabbit's.

2

The circus has had to park on the tarmac because there is no space in the park, as the local authority preferred to give the licence to an Indian community celebrating some strange festival.

Every afternoon I go out on the balcony and see the children stuffing their mouths with sugar before running around with plastic flags; the mothers stand about, eating and adjusting their purple and golden garments – from their faces it looks more like a funeral than a festival.

In the evening I have to close the window despite the heat because I don't know how else to protect myself from the noise, but the music gets in under the glass anyway; I think I know some of the songs by heart now, although I don't know anyone Indian, who could tell me whether I'm getting the words wrong.

Aurelio asked if I wanted to go and see the snakes and I said yes, because the funfair rides are close to the circus and I want to say hello to my friend who sets them up.

Aurelio doesn't know him, we've been dating for a week and we don't talk much about the past.

While I am having a shower before going out my mother comes into the bathroom and starts giving me a summary of what's been happening in a TV soap; I ask her if she could put out her cigarette because the bathroom is the only room where I can get away from that smell.

"Our life would have been much easier if you'd started smoking as well," she says, breaking off the tip of the Marlboro, throwing it into her cup, and keeping the rest.

"And who would have paid for them?" I ask from behind the curtain that I wash with bleach to get rid of the limescale.

I hear her put the toilet seat down, to sit on it, while I wait for a bit to soak in a coconut conditioner that according to the hairdresser will revive my hair in ways I cannot even imagine, and as a matter of fact after a month I still can't.

Instead of replying she says that every woman is entitled to two great love affairs in her life, the Argentinian soaps are right about that. At one time we used to watch them together when I came home from school, but since I gave up bookkeeping sitting down to eat that early depresses me, so I always try to have something else to do.

A job for instance, and Aurelio says he has a solution to that too.

"Are you going out with your fella this evening?" she asks while I'm plucking my eyebrows.

When I don't reply she pinches my arm and I stamp my foot, watching her in the mirror; my mother is not afraid to laugh even though in place of teeth she has brown and blackened crevices.

I put down the tweezers to check whether at least this time I've done them evenly; once I almost plucked the whole lot out by mistake and my father started calling me "the alien".

I ask Ma whether she remembers, and she laughs at the thought of how ugly I looked.

"Fortunately they grew back," she says, pulling my hair back behind my ears, then she adopts that serious look that comes over her when she is watching soaps, and tells me to be careful because it is better to spend fifteen euros on the pill than fifty on baby food.

I put on a pair of jeans to cover my mosquito-ravaged legs; every summer I vow not to scratch myself and instead it only gets worse. When I was a kid I couldn't have any scabs or they would have shown up in the dance recital photos, so I would bite my fingernails down to the quick as it was impossible to scratch myself with my fingertips.

Now I don't need my legs to be perfect except to make love, and Aurelio and I haven't got to that point yet.

When I step out of the main door Aurelio is squeezing an insect bite between his fingers, complaining about the heat. "One thing's for sure, if it starts like this, it's going to be an infernal summer."

We walk to the circus and on the way we stop at the stalls selling jelly sweets; he fills a bag with the ones I like and when I pull out a ten-euro note he gives me a pat on the cheek and tells me not to be daft.

In front of the serpentarium there is a girl lifting a slimy black reptile out of a basket, she wraps it round her neck and then remains completely motionless until they appear to be a single entity. Aurelio stares at her and bares his teeth. I haven't yet got used to so much of his gums showing: when he kisses me his lips suddenly draw back and I never know what to do with all that space. At a certain point the girl notices us and asks if he wants to touch the snake, and while Aurelio strokes it I tell him I'm going to say hello to a friend – he nods and reminds me to check my mobile.

The guy on the fairground rides, Renato and I know each other from when he used to let me have rides for free every time his parents parked their camper van in the park near my apartment block.

Renato went on the road with them only in the summer to avoid missing school; my father once repaired the camper van they travelled in and after our parents hit it off with each other we were encouraged to be friends because they were afraid our shyness might be a sign of homosexuality and sociopathy.

As a kid I even fancied Renato, but to tease me his sisters told me not to bother because he was gay. "Can't you see he wears an earring in his right ear?" And I nodded, knowing what they were getting at.

As soon as he recognises me among the people waiting in line, he gives the signal to stop and helps two children out of their car.

When he hugs me I notice he has more of a paunch than before and he is wearing the same supermarket aftershave. "You've had your braces removed", "You've coloured your hair", "You've put on a few kilos", "I can't believe you're eighteen," he says without waiting for a reply.

A loudspeaker announces the start of the ride and the cars begin to move around behind us; I turn round and see Aurelio on the other side of the road, he sits down on the step of a booth beside the snake girl. The snake has disappeared.

I can't see his gums from here, whenever he makes another woman laugh he seems more manly.

"I'm with someone," I say, pointing to him.

"Do you want a ride?" asks Renato without taking any notice of what I am saying.

"I got my driving licence."

"And you're still alive?"

I put my hand out for a token but he says I don't need one, they're state-of-the-art cars.

When I go on the bumper cars I always drive at strangers, I make sweeping manoeuvres to gain speed, then I spin round a few times and swoop into the centre of the ring, crashing into anybody, and making them jump in their seats. I like looking them in the face when it happens, turning round with an apologetic look and carrying on in the same way.

Sometimes I like to have a go on my own – Renato used to let me when there were no customers and summer was turning into those empty rides in the sun, with disco music that brought women out onto their balconies, the sky dissolving behind electoral posters for candidates from a distant past.

I tell Renato I haven't got time for another go but we can have lunch together the next day, even though I don't want to talk about my father's arrest and I know his parents are curious to find out what he has been up to.

I do a few dance steps and bend my knees to show him I am still supple. Renato tries to copy me, to the music coming from the loudspeakers, but he immediately feels embarrassed and asks if I still think about dancing.

"As ever, but I had an accident," I reply, rotating the ankle that I broke some years ago during a dance recital. Then I walk away, backwards so I can continue to wave to him.

When I rejoin Aurelio, he is still talking to the girl from the serpentarium.

She has red hair, a shade that you see on the boxes of those do-it-yourself hair-dye kits. She must be naturally fair because they don't normally turn out like that: I know because when I was a teenager I tried being many things, but my hair wouldn't hold the colour and the ammonia made my ears itch.

"Are you happy to do a Tarot reading?" asks Aurelio, and for a moment I think he has got me confused with my mother, who before going to bed at night shakes the I-Ching coins in the coffee cups and then turns them over on to the tablecloth to see what is going to become of us.

"I'll do it for free," says the girl. "I'm learning, it's still a hobby."

We follow her into the trailer where she sleeps; when she opens the door the first thing I notice is the smell of mentholated talcum powder that you put in your gym shoes so that they don't smell.

I look at her feet. She is wearing a pair of dirty combat boots with the laces undone: shoes that are totally unsuitable for this weather. For a moment I envy her the freedom to make that choice.

"You can't come in," she says to Aurelio, giving him a shove to send him away. "Go for a walk, come back in fifteen minutes."

I am embarrassed but the girl draws me by the elbow and sits me down on a stool, then takes a deck of cards from a drawer in her camper kitchen. Instead of turning on the light she uses a couple of stubby white candles, the kind they put in churches to get fifty cents out of you when you're feeling sorry for someone who has died or for all the illnesses you are yet to succumb to. "Cut the pack with your left hand and don't touch anything else," she orders before laying the cards out in three straight lines. After she has turned them over one at a time, she asks me to wait a few minutes.

The moonlight filtering through the blinds is blocked by Aurelio's cheek as he tries to spy on what is going on in the trailer; I shake my head to send him away and the girl says: "Yeah, it's really negative."

What she feels when she takes hold of my hands: if I don't control my energy, I will end up setting apartments on fire, causing lightbulbs to explode and locusts to emerge from storm drains, and only twins to be born.

The girl continues to recite a series of prophecies and I can't think of anything to say.

When we come out of the trailer she asks Aurelio if he wants a reading but he says it's late, then he takes me by the hand and we walk slowly across the tarmac until we get back to the Fiat 600 which he has parked below my place.

"You want to go somewhere quiet?" he asks, and I understand the moment has come.

We stop in an open space with hardly any light from the street lamps and he touches me until there's no breath in my mouth left and it is nothing like the first kiss I gave to a schoolmate, from which I got nothing but a taste of saliva and vinegar.

I continue to keep my eyes fixed on him even when he's

hurting me and Aurelio says I'm like a cat in the dark.

No one has ever told me that before – I don't have light-coloured eyes – and I don't know what to say so I wrap my legs round his back and stretch out more comfortably on the car seat even though the velour irritates my skin, and I feel supple and hot and invincible.

Before he drops me off Aurelio asks me what the Tarot reader said.

"That I'm special," I reply with a smile now straightened by braces.

"Don't lie to me," he says, pinching my hips. "I can tell."

The day after I lost my virginity, an underground water pipe bursts in the open space where the circus is, and they come and put up notices in the apartment block to inform us of the problem.

In the afternoon, when the heat is about to make the windows melt, the circus hands actually come round making door to door calls because they have used up all their reserves. A lad asks me if we can bring some water and watering cans, and so I stand in line beneath a chalk-coloured sky along with my mother, who is carrying the biggest pasta pot we have: it is like a procession but she says it is just an excuse to make us feel sorry for them and to sell tickets.

When I approach a cage following the instructions of a girl in trapeze artist's tights, the monkey I am supposed to water is holed up in a corner and I don't know what to do to get it to come out.

Before going off, the girl tells me to avoid making sudden movements and childish noises, so I confine myself to dipping my hand in the pot, then slipping it between the bars and trying to sprinkle water over the animal, but the water disappears, absorbed by the straw and by the heat. However, the monkey comes nearer, so I reach out my arm as far as I can to pour water between its lips – a process that is awkward for both of us. After a bit my legs hurt and I crouch down beside the cage, getting used to the smell; I blow bubbles with my chewing gum to attract the monkey's attention and to find out whether it is capable of laughing, until the girl comes back to thank me and tells me I can go now. When I get home the sun turns purple and red, an eyeball with broken blood vessels. Aurelio is right: this summer the heat is going to be murderous.

3

"Cut it off."

"Are you sure?"

Catherine gets out of the hammock she has attached to the balcony railings; she bought it in a wholesale supermarket that sells soap bubble mixture and beach umbrellas.

The apartment she shares with her mother is on the eighth floor of a block that was built in the '70s, all the interiors are a mixture of marble, brass and newspaper.

On days when she is not working at the hotel she spends longer shampooing her hair and lies in the hammock to let it dry in the sun and from that height she contrives to swing in empty space, cutting out from view the encrustation of electric cables on the green-painted walls and the efflorescence tattooed on the rendering.

The next-door neighbour has complained about the proliferation of a bougainvillea over her railings and Caterina's mother has promised to deal with the problem: after the arrest of her husband many years ago, she gave up the freedom of eccentric behaviour and never raises any protest in residents' association meetings.

"I've had it since I got married," she says when Caterina cuts off a bit of the plant with some clippers. She is talking to the cat in her arms, not to her daughter.

When they were first married her husband used to give her flowers, then he started bringing her packets of seeds to grow all sorts of things. For him it was an imaginative gesture, for her just another way to spend less.

"Should I cut those off as well or leave them like that?" Caterina asks her mother, pointing at a tuft of leaves on the climber. Not getting a reply, she begins to cut them with a serrated knife, the texture of the plant under the blade is fibrous like that of cooked meat.

"We've no more space, you've got to get rid of some clothes," is what her mother says, however.

For some months now she has been filling the apartment with ferns, which reduce the oxygen available for anyone asleep – it is her way of hinting that Caterina should move out.

"You've got to live your own life, you can't live like me,' she insists, but she is still talking to the cat.

Caterina once got a rose thorn embedded in her hand and she couldn't get it out. She said nothing about it for a week, until the wound forced out a sliver of wood and she was left with a cut that was not suppurating but would not close up either, like the stigmata.

Her mother tried to convince her she was a witch, she had started to think she was a saint. Now, when anyone asks her about the scar in the middle of her palm, she says it is just an extended life line.

"And where am I to go?" she replies before being interrupted by the telephone ringing.

"It's him again," her mother shouts from the sitting room. Caterina brushes the earth from her jeans as she re-enters the apartment.

"Has he hung up?" she asks, having whispered to her not to shout.

"No, he's still on the line."

Caterina takes the cordless phone and falls back on her bed, hoping her voice sounds languid and sexy. A few days ago she destroyed her mobile plugging it into a faulty socket in the hotel and she has not got the money to replace it; she would rather not use the Siemens Aurelio gave her long ago as a birthday present except in an emergency. If she gets messages on it, the characters are too big and too spaced out, and don't look genuine.

"So, what happened?" the policeman asks her. "Did you break it?"

"No, someone put the evil eye on it."

"I thought you'd be asleep, I remembered you were on night duty."

"That hotel is worse than a police station."

"What are you talking about?"

"I swear it. Yesterday night a guest asked me if he could use the phone to speak to his wife who won't let him see his daughter; he asked me if I'd pretend to be his lover and help him to play a trick on her."

Caterina was about to refuse, then she checked the guest's name on the register and discovered he had been sleeping in the hotel for ten days, so she dialled a number scrawled on a scrap of paper, hoping no one would answer.

"And what did the wife say to you?"

The woman had listened while Caterina explained she would not be getting her husband back, and only when a child asked to have the cartoon channel changed did she hang up.

"That they're always the perfect boyfriend for the first six months."

"And then what did you do?"

"I got a couple of the sleeping pills that had been found in bedside tables and gave them to him."

"Poor guy."

"Poor me, that phone call destroyed my mobile."

No sooner had Caterina plugged it in to recharge it than there was a sudden blue flash from the wall socket and she hadn't been able to use it since. Afterwards she had thrown away all the sleeping pills hotel guests had forgotten to take with them, medications whose expiry dates she had never bothered to check.

"I have to buy a birthday present for my mother, do you want to come? This evening we can eat out with some friends of mine," says the policeman and his voice delves into her spine.

He has never wanted to introduce her to anyone before now.

A few hours later Caterina is waiting for him at the traffic lights near the Tiburtina bridge that leads into the newly renovated station; she is distracted and jostled by passers-by until the tarmac starts to shake and everybody stops dead, trying to remember where they were the last time there was an earthquake. "They've been saying for a hundred years that this bridge is about to collapse," a man exclaims.

When the light turns red the cars drive over it anyway and no one disappears between the cracks, catastrophe having already been absorbed by the sticky black bitumen.

For a few seconds the vibration of the earth seemed to Caterina reassuring.

"Where are we going?" she asks the policeman as soon as she gets into the car.

"Ostia. Someone recommended a place there that sells statues," he replies, lowering the window. The wind catches her hair, causing it to flutter in front of her face; Caterina tries to disentangle it, looking at herself in the rear-view mirror, but the policeman catches her hand and stops her.

"I like it when your hair's ruffled."

"My mother wants a statue of St Francis," he explains later to the shop assistant and Caterina starts to wander among the stone frogs and saints, hoping to find one with an expression that is not too severe. When she spots one in restrained colours that the policeman likes too, she wonders whether he will tell his mother she helped him choose it, but he does not talk much about his feelings, just as he doesn't discuss his sense of guilt for not having become a special unit officer like his brother who was stabbed to death.

Once she had opened his wallet to get out a condom and her hand had brushed the shiny and much-fingered face of a guy who looked like him, with the smile of someone who shows off their scars rather than covers them up.

Caterina had not asked him about it because it was the kind of photo you see in cemeteries or on the news.

Having put the statue in the boot of the car, they go for a walk on the beach and she is ashamed of her feet, the distorted bones showing up against the sand. In some places the skin is so thin you can see the actual colour of her veins.

"I'm sorry, dancing has ruined them," she confesses, blurting it out before he notices them.

"They look nice anyway," he replies without paying much attention.

Now and again the policeman stops to pick up bits of glass while he talks about extinct marine species and plankton.

"You know a lot."

"I wanted to study biology after I left school. I was good enough," he went on without giving her time to comment, "but no one really noticed. Even as a boy I was an infiltrator."

After a while he opens her hand and slips the warm, smooth-edged pieces of glass into her hand; she puts one over her eye to look through it and her vision splinters into crystals.

"Thanks."

"Every so often I do something nice."

Caterina takes his arm, surprised by her disquiet, and for a while she walks with her eyes closed – beneath her eyelids she sees sun spots and constellations that dissolve, then break up and bleed into each other, and her stride becomes looser and more relaxed.

"You can find another job if you don't like working at the hotel," says the policeman.

"I know," she replies without opening her eyes.

"It's not your fault."

"I never thought it was. For me, it's nobody's fault."

What Caterina likes about afternoons in Ostia are the ash-blue huts and the smell of bricks, and the feel of crushed shells under her feet and the row of empty houses at the end of the season, when the sky is almost transparent and no one around her has any pretensions to being an occasional fisherman or having a special affinity with the sea.

They go to Fiumicino to eat because it is smarter and the policeman's colleagues like the boats.

They have chosen a place she has been to many times with Aurelio's family; his parents had a fish shop and this was one of the restaurants they supplied.

At the desk she is careful not to stand too close to the policeman while the owner checks the details of the booking without looking up from the register.

As soon as he sees her he gets up and hugs her as if she were his goddaughter.

"Don't worry, leave it to me. Choose what you want and we'll see to the rest," he exclaims, pointing to the fish lying on ice.

Caterina picks out one, having examined it carefully; the owner pinches her cheek, complimenting her on her choice and the policeman's colleagues notice her existence.

She hasn't called Aurelio's mother in a month but at that moment she is thankful to her for having taught her to distinguish a glassy eye from a healthy one.

"You've been here often?" the policeman asks her when they sit down.

Caterina worked in Aurelio's family's fish shop for six months and cleaned so many fish her skin was covered with silver scales.

"Yes, it's a family place."

"I'm sorry, I didn't know," he says, taking her hand under the table while she observes the girlfriends of the other policemen. They are a bit common – Caterina is never that.

One of them admires her make-up and asks if it's good to use rice powder as an exfoliant; another asks her the name of the powder blush she has put on her cheeks – Kamikaze Pink.

As she fillets the fish she notices that some of the girls have badly applied nail polish with lots of ridges on their nails; to overcome her embarrassment she spends the rest of the meal giving advice on what varnishes and solvents to use.

When the policeman gets up to go to the bathroom the guy sitting beside him moves next to Caterina and explains that he is a union official, employed to defend the rights of those working in that sector.

She wants him to like her, she has always had a reverential respect for anyone who manages to become a union official.

"How did you two meet?" he asks her.

"Caterina had a show on," the policeman cuts in as he takes his seat again.

In fact at that point she was already working as a stripper.

"I studied ballet for seven years, then I started choreographing for a nightclub.

"And did you dance as well?" asks the girl sitting beside her. Her eyelashes are separated with clear mascara, the type that does not run if you cry. "Sometimes," Caterina replies, without mentioning the incident that left her with a hip that crumbles on contact. When someone starts talking about food again, and the policeman and the union official are discussing the effect of traffic on feelings of personal frustration, she continues to explain that foundation should be applied with the fingers because the brushes sold by sales promoters in shopping centres spread bacteria.

At the end of the meal, when the sugar at the bottom of the coffee cups has become a sticky paste and no one wants to make a move lest it offend the others, she is expected to share a couple's enthusiasm for a trip to Bali.

With all their talk of grey and violent waves that could kill tourists, Caterina is bored.

"Show us a few dance moves," says one of the policeman's colleagues when they go to a nightclub near the restaurant, but she only dances on request when she is on stage.

She joins the policeman and orders a fluorescent cocktail, leaning against the bar while he strokes her skin beneath her top; when the music is turned down she hears a couple on the divan talking about a Thai village where the people use leech therapy.

Once she went to an erotic trade fair with a dancer she had become friendly with; Caterina wanted to buy costumes, the other girl wanted to learn new ways of getting herself tied up.

They were at a bondage stand run by women only, who were busy reassuring clients about the hygiene of their products, when her friend pointed to a table covered with electric cables and ampoules, across the aisle. "They look like what a beautician uses to oxygenate the skin." Glass insects that purify the skin without bleeding it.

They went over to the owner of the stand and discovered that the equipment was actually a pleasure machine that predated the invention of pornography on video-cassette; you simply applied the electrodes to specific parts of the body and raised the voltage to produce a sensation akin to an orgasm.

When the man put a suction cup behind her ear the dancer remained impassive, then she burst out laughing, lamenting her cynicism; Caterina, however, had to ask him to turn the machine off straightaway. As soon as the light connected to the electrodes came on she emitted a long and clammy moan that came far too easily.

The girlfriend of one of the policemen, who was almost knocked unconscious by a hurricane in Bali, complains about her job in a hospital and says that Rome is impossible; someone replies, "This city brutalises only those who don't understand it."

Caterina sits next to the policeman and reaches across the table to pour the remains of a bottle of prosecco into her glass; the union guy asks whether the place where she dances was one of the night spots targeted by the police in an operation that earned their bosses promotion and drove the press into a state of hysteria that lasted for weeks.

"Not only that, she was going out with one of the guys we arrested," says the policeman, leaning his head back on the divan and pulling Caterina towards him.

"Are you enjoying yourself?" he asks her, kissing her ear. She nods with a repeated, hypnotic movement of her head.

"You're crazy. Do they know you're in a relationship with a witness?" exclaims the union guy.

"The investigation's over."

"Not at all. If they want to they can even close down my cousin's pizzeria; once the big places have gone, it's all the others next."

The policeman stands up, unsteadily and wearily, and with a wave of his hand that is lost in the dark he says, "We'll talk about it another time."

"You told me you're never allowed to tell anybody anything, that it's classified information. Why did you tell him about me and Aurelio?" asks Caterina in the car.

"He's a friend."

"How involved are you in the whole operation?"

The policeman starts to laugh.

"What?"

"The way you say *operation* makes me laugh."

"That's what they call it in the newspapers."

"Oh well, in that case," he teases her, pinching her arm.

"You know what I mean."

"I know who I am supposed to question and who I am supposed to handcuff, the rest the others do."

"Are you just saying that to pacify me."

He continues to laugh, shaking his head. "It's a bit late for that."

"Aurelio thinks someone snitched on him and the police took advantage."

At that point the policeman lets go of the gearstick to take her hand; Caterina remains silent, staring at the green nimbus round the moon until it leaves a circle imprinted on her retina.

The policeman starts singing to himself on the stairs leading to his apartment; Caterina takes the keys from his back pocket and runs on ahead.

When he comes in he pretends to chase after her and she flees towards the bedroom giggling like a child, then they embrace and both of them begin shouting even though someone is banging on the wall.

While they are lying there still with their clothes on, he

runs his finger along her nose.

"You've got freckles and black hair, the two don't go together."

"I'm abnormal," Caterina smiles, revealing a dimple in her left cheek.

"And you have only one dimple instead of two."

"I told you, I have strange genes," she says, her smile broadening even more.

"What's more, your mouth's crooked."

"That's not true."

"It's just that no one's ever had the guts to tell you."

"Where?" asks Caterina, going up to the mirror facing the bed.

"You can't tell," the policeman says, coming up behind her, "it happens when you laugh. This bit here twists to the right, and you look as if you're grimacing even though you're happy."

"Then I believe it," says Caterina, before removing her top in silence.

"And I'm also dyslexic," she tells him, pushing him back on to the mattress.

The place is sealed with mosquito screens and double glazing so all that can be heard is the vibration of the household appliances and the sound of their breathing; the policeman turns over during the stage when dreams begin to invade consciousness like bubbles of ink rising to the surface of water and he presses against her hip, the one Aurelio broke when he slammed her against a wall.

Caterina moans, quietly so as not to wake him, and turns

on the plasma screen mounted in front of the bed; the voice of the presenter of a scientific programme is a barely audible intrusion, describing desert plants capable of surviving the most hostile of environments, shrubs that with barely a drop of water explode into bloom, or in the absence of rain dry up and retract their own roots, awaiting the first generous winds of the season.

4

We were little more than twenty years old, Aurelio, Marco and I, when we decided to open a nightclub.

In those days we would go round Rome looking for ideas and we always came home on the night bus to avoid being fined for drunk driving or getting into arguments with car park attendants.

Aurelio would complain that he wanted something different, but the only thing we learned from the places we went to was that we liked bar staff who came from abroad and that we could transform gambling into something elegant.

"Nothing like the Bingo halls full of rose vendors."

We actually went to a Bingo hall to pick up Aurelio's grandmother who blew her pension on bingo cards; the rest of the money she gave to an unscrupulous hairdresser who instead of persuading her to keep her hair white sent her home with bright colour rinses that stained the bath and clashed with her clothes.

"She's entitled to feel young," the hairdresser told us when we explained to him the old lady could not afford to have a blow-dry every week.

His grandmother's favourite Bingo hall – the one near Porta Maggiore – had heavy-duty carpeting and smelled strongly of airline food, but the ladies at the table and who she sat with, were kind and never cheated her even though she was not very good at playing.

"When are you going to accept the fact you're eighty years old?" Aurelio's mother would say to her mother-in-law, who to spite her would take another pair of earrings to the Cash for Gold shop. With all the money she had acquired there, she had got herself a reputation for being a gypsy princess.

Aurelio, Marco and I were not afraid of the people outside the stations: if a bus driver refused to let drunken lads get on we would act like nighttime law enforcers and embarrass him in front of everybody, but we were shocked by the social isolation of those who would harm themselves just to spend a night in the warmth, behind bars or in hospital.

For us the nightclub should be a place that would lift your feet off the ground and have you on your knees when you came out; we wanted people to lose track of time, to forget, to spend money like water.

We did not find any places like that; at the weekend we would go dancing on Via Ostiense to learn which were the best DJs and how easy it was to empty the dance floor with the wrong song, in overheated venues in breach of safety regulations that made me feel claustrophobic, so Mario would yell out I was pregnant, I'd pretend to faint and with Aurelio supporting me, with his hand on my back, we would go off laughing, leaving people wondering what kind of mother I would be.

We even went to clubs in Porta Maggiore, where heroin addicts lurking in the gaps between buildings would be caught in the neon lights, places all mirrors and velvet where guys would stand around looking bored and instead of dancing would stick to the walls like spiders or do kung fu moves to music that made them feel even more depressed; or those glittery places near Termini station, full of South Americans, where it was impossible to order a cocktail without pineapple in it.

Going past the Rossana guest houses and the Caput Mundi hotels, we would suddenly stop to look at the faded sky above Via Giolitti, but perhaps it was just because we were excited and walking past the nougat sellers submerged in artificial lighting we felt as if we were on holiday. Aurelio said, "White bats," pointing to the birds flying overhead, although they were only seagulls.

To learn how to open a nightclub we had even ended up in a club on Via del Mare at the suggestion of someone Mario knew, and before we got to Acilia we commented on the apartment blocks being built near the road.

"There are no supermarkets. Or shops. There are no squares. There's nothing," said Mario, comparing life in those places to assisted suicide.

Those apartment blocks that we could see from the road were beehives without the bees, and in the diffuse humid light of the traffic they looked like those abandoned temples that every so often are rediscovered in the jungle.

"But some of the apartment blocks have swimming pools

and there are loads of cinemas," I observed as we drove past publicity hoardings for wedding venues or playgrounds.

And then there were the nightclubs, although it was complicated finding them; Mario's contact had given him the correct address but we had to drive up and down the same roads lined with suburban houses and lit by orange street lamps before we found it. Having left the car in a private parking zone, I started peering into the windows of the houses – almost all of them had a garden with those white and pink flowers that you see along motorways, and there was that seemingly sweet smell of linden in the air that suddenly becomes unpleasant, as if you had sniffed detergent.

For the owners it was strange seeing a girl among the clientele, but they let us in anyway and every time a stripper came too close Aurelio held my hand; I lowered my head so as not to see who was touching her.

The strippers and I, we had the same fake tears you can stick on by your eyes, but those girls were smooth in places I didn't even know it was possible to be.

That evening I realised that a nightclub has to have the same lighting as an aquarium; it is easier to plumb the depths if, when you see yourself in the mirror, you look like a mermaid – a creature that doesn't exist.

We had actually spoken of our plans to my father, who was changing tyres in Abruzzo and in his earlier life had been subjected to hundreds of tax inspections; he had been in prison but we still trusted his advice.

"Think about it carefully, even if you're legit those places attract some unsavoury types." It would have been easy to make some catty response, but we didn't.

My mother and I saw little of him and only if we went to visit him up in the mountains.

After his release he moved to a village where there wasn't even a petrol station and the only two bars kept reporting each other for violations of building regulations about which the forces of law and order were unable to express an opinion.

Sometimes I'd wonder why I wasn't able to make him fancy me: if he'd been attracted to girls at my school who were younger than me, if he was sick – as someone said – why hadn't he looked at me in that way?

It was wrong to think like that, and I only confessed that I had to Aurelio. He stared at me in a strange way before telling me that even though it was a difficult period I would come out of it stronger than before.

But I thought it even when I went to see him at Rebibbia and I made an effort to look good to make him proud of me, but it was only the guards who noticed my straight toned legs.

Having been round all those discos and chatted at the bars with students who went on about university exams that were unbelievably boring, Aurelio, Mario and I were just over twenty and we still didn't know how to open a nightclub.

Getting a licence was too difficult so we decided to try a video rental franchise, although as usual I didn't have enough money to contribute.

They set up shop in a former haberdashery in Torpignattara, where we spent the afternoons eating popcorn from the automatic vending machine by the door, waiting for clients who wanted to rent horror films or crime movies. In fact people who didn't want to rent anything also came in and stayed to talk about supposed knifings or criminal gangs that we had never seen; one of our problems was our belief that the gentlemen who called on us asking for protection money for the shop were not racketeers but missionaries.

Some of those who asked for protection money, I liked: they'd have lunch in the only two family-run trattorias left in the street, they wore suede bomber jackets over polo shirts and declared themselves to be racist only towards foreigners who were adults.

Having confused us with pictures of their grandchildren and suggestions about how to avoid the high rents that had supposedly engulfed Rome like quicksands, they always asked us for a contribution to bolster security in the neighbourhood.

"You never know what might happen: a load of rubbish dumped in front of your shutters, a burnt mattress out the back, cars destroyed. Some people are unpredictable," they would say with a weak smile, without ever making it clear who they were talking about, and with vague references to a mosque in the area.

I didn't take much notice, although Mario and Aurelio were becoming ever more impatient and told me not to let them in when it was my turn to be on the till and I'd listen to music with headphones on to cover the sound of the local train that wheezed like a person with no vocal cords despite the fact the carriages on this route had been changed a short while ago.

I liked that neighbourhood, especially when we closed a bit early and went for a walk alongside the tracks as far as the railway-workers' cottages near the aqueduct, in the late-spring evenings when the city smelt of tarmac and mint.

My favourite customer was a lady I grew fond of because she didn't understand a thing about the films she rented. She liked long films in costume, so I recommended the DVD of *Cleopatra*. When she came back, she told us she liked it because the Queen of Egypt had brought down the Roman Empire and then Aurelio insisted on watching it, but he fell asleep halfway through. When he asked me how it ended, I had to explain to him the lady was wrong: that film was like my mother's soap operas, the ones in which every woman has two great loves and is too stupid not to die on account of them, except it was made in Hollywood instead of Argentina.

The dancers I met after Aurelio and Marco opened the nightclub were shocked by my innocence: some of them had started stripping at the age of fourteen, in towns I'd never even heard of.

At that age I was still studying ballet in a school that allowed us a discount on the monthly fees because my mother helped out, cleaning the room where we practised.

When she didn't make me do my homework, I'd go with her on the pretext of helping her to sweep the floor, but actually I wanted to do the exercises without the teacher and the other girls in the class.

Although my father had left and we were living on our own, our house was always full of things and I had to allow the detritus of their marriage even in the room where I slept.

Behind my winter jackets were the high-waisted trousers and psychedelic-print shirts they'd worn when they were courting, and that now looked like carnival costumes.

Maybe that's why I've always liked being in gymnasiums and in the parish halls where we did catechism; they were big empty spaces where I could play on my own and do dance steps unimpeded, before the others arrived to talk about God or abs.

While I'd be bending backwards till I could touch the floor my mother would be mopping it, telling me to get out of the way, but we were both happy because the classical music calmed us even if we didn't say so out loud.

The girls at the nightclub often talked about the mafia or cosmetic surgery centres, but when I looked for pictures of their home towns on the internet all I saw were domed buildings with tarnished cupolas or wooden cabins in which you could get drunk while having a sauna.

"That's the nice part," they would say. "Try kissing someone who hasn't a single tooth in his head."

The clientele was young and high-spirited and the girls were happy, which meant that at a certain point Mario was convinced he'd saved them.

Aurelio on the other hand felt a bit ashamed and tried to explain to his parents what burlesque was, even though that wasn't exactly what the girls did in the nightclub, but the word *circus* put his mother's mind at rest: when she sought reassurance from me about our night life, I kept it vague and asked her to help me choose costumes for the shows.

One day I took her to a shop in Esquilino where they sold sequined camisoles half price and she went home with plastic bags full of bracelets and tiaras for the grandchildren's Christmas presents.

5

By the windows of the women's section of the prison Caterina sees a car with the boot open and stereo subwoofers resting inside the spare wheels. The vehicle belongs to some volunteers from an association promoting quality of life at Rebibbia, guys with partially shaved heads and asymmetric haircuts who raise the volume of the stereo on request and smile when they chat with the woman at the windows, trying to tell from their dialects where they come from.

While she bends down to tie her shoe laces, Caterina looks up towards the prison and sees the women with their backs to the windows, leaning against the bars, smoking and touching their necks – in the early afternoon light, they are dark and noisy.

When she comes into the visiting room Aurelio has a softened expression she is no longer used to.

"You look cheerful," she says, leaning forward to get a better look at him and find out whether there's anything else that's different.

"I've spoken to the lawyer; they're letting me out within a month."

Aurelio's teeth are regular and thin to the point they seem almost transparent; in prison they have taken on a yellowish tinge that makes his smile more human.

"What's happened?" she asks, before remembering to smile.

"They can't keep me in on the basis of the evidence they've got, the dancers' statements are too contradictory. Some have said they went with clients on their own initiative and that Mario and I didn't profit at all from it."

"Sex in return for payment is a crime regardless of who pockets the money. What did they arrest you for otherwise?"

"That's their problem. I paid them to dance."

"So soon then, within a month?"

"What do you mean, soon? That's thirty days…"

"I don't feel the same as I did before," says Caterina.

The music coming from the volunteers' stereo is too far away from the men's prison section, so she can hear the ringing of a mobile phone belonging to a guard who doesn't have to leave his personal belongings in the lockers.

"Of course not, since I've been inside I don't feel the same as before either."

"I'm pleased you're getting out."

"I should hope so," says Aurelio biting his lip.

"But I don't know how things will turn out for the two of us."

"In what sense?"

"As a couple."

"What?"

"Don't laugh," says Caterina.

"It seems strange you should be telling me this now," he replies.

"Please don't laugh."

A guard approaches where they are sitting, he's young and she's never seen him before.

"You said you'd wait," says Aurelio in a low voice so as not to be overheard.

"When did I say that? You took it for granted."

"Look at me," Aurelio whispers.

Caterina stares at the guy in uniform, he must be boiling in those shoes – who knows whether he was given them along with the uniform and whether he comes to the prison already dressed like that.

Some of the strippers at the nightclub preferred to sleep till late and when they turned up for work they already had on their glittery costumes underneath their fleeces and pyjamas; they would go out on stage soft and sweaty with sleep, in a state of drowsiness that made them even more inscrutable and sensual.

"Hey, I'm still here," Aurelio says to her.

"Sorry, my contact lenses are bothering me in this light."

"There's something else I've got to tell you," he says, trying to get as close as possible to her.

"It's all happening today."

"Remember how I was before they arrested me?"

"I don't want to talk about it."

"You remember I was always on edge?"

"Yes," Caterina replies, without mentioning how much

the painkillers for her hip that he'd broken had cost her.

"And we had less and less money? I never told you we were being blackmailed."

"Who by?"

"They don't leave visiting cards. They wanted a share of the takings from Mario and me, otherwise they'd start saying we were exploiting the dancers and forcing them to prostitute themselves."

"Since when?" she asks.

"Six months before they closed us down. We always paid up to avoid problems, then the police came to check us out."

"Why didn't you tell me before?'

"It was better not to," Aurelio replies.

"Does your mother know?"

"What do you think?"

"And your brother?" Caterina presses him.

"You think I wanted to look like an idiot?"

"No, but perhaps you were naive."

"Why is it, I'm the one that's in prison and you're the one that's tetchy?"

Caterina moves her chair back even though visiting time is not yet over.

"What's the point of telling me now?" she asks.

"I thought perhaps you could talk to the policeman who arrested me; perhaps he realises there's something odd about the investigation. Now that I'm coming out I can even file a complaint, the lawyer says."

"Aurelio, there's nothing odd about it. Why would he want to get involved? Anyway I don't know him."

"But they're still questioning you, aren't they? If you're a witness you can talk to him, you can call him."

"How would you know whether they're still questioning me?"

"My brother went by your place to drop off a parcel and he saw you in the car with him; he met him at the police station. I'm sorry they're not leaving you alone."

"I'm sorry, my eyes are dry. I can't keep them open, I keep wanting to rub them."

"Stop it, they're all red."

"I can't," says Caterina, closing them again and rubbing them hard.

Aurelio would grab her hands to stop her but he knows the guard would be over before he had time to touch her.

"Caterina, I'll be out soon, but I could have ended up not here, in prison. I don't know whether you realise, but I'm here just because it suited somebody and that's not fair."

"The drug dealing isn't something they made up."

"I've never touched the stuff."

"Aurelio."

"Don't look at me like that, not even you could help laughing," says Aurelio with a smile.

"Well, I'm not."

"I could have done things differently. When they blackmailed me I agreed to pay instead of going to the police."

"Anyone would have done the same."

"I don't know. I wouldn't do the same today."

"Now you're going to tell me you've changed?"

Aurelio starts laughing and shakes his head at her.

"I don't know what's come over you lately," he says.

"I'll get myself arrested now, too: perhaps I'll become a

Buddhist and calm down."

"It's all for the best," remarks Aurelio, giving her a long look. "I've been thinking about it; being in Rebibbia has been like doing a year in the army, it doesn't change anything."

"I don't know."

"Do you remember, my father wanted me to join the army instead of opening a nightclub? Well, I've made him happy," says Aurelio, shrugging his shoulders, and at that moment, touched by his self-deprecating smile, Caterina feels she hates him with such unexpected ferocity she could scratch his face.

"Who knows where I would have ended up," he insists. "You were right, Mario wasn't good for me."

"It's my fault as well, I should have noticed sooner."

"You're beautiful."

"What?"

"I like your hair like that. You look older."

Caterina touches the strands of her neat black bob cut just above the shoulder, she has not had her hair so short since she was at secondary school. Strippers never have short hair, unless they wear synthetic wigs which they whip off when the show is about to end.

"It doesn't change anything, Caterina."

"You can't tell," she replies.

"I know you don't feel the same as before."

"All right. I've got to go."

"It's just a matter of time."

"Don't think about it now."

"Will you be here again on Thursday?"

"Yes."

As soon as she comes out of the room she realises that her

top has become soaked through with sweat during the visit – her fruit-scented powdered deodorant does not last two hours.

A girl hands her a leaflet on the failings of repressive institutions in Italy; the ink on the photocopy is still fresh and when Caterina takes it she is left with black marks on her fingertips, then she uses it to fan her face.

"Are you OK?" asks the girl.

"It's hard," she continues when Caterina nods without speaking. "Who have you got inside?"

"My boyfriend."

"Will he have to stay long?"

"He's coming out in a month."

"That's good news."

The girl moves closer to put a hand on her shoulder and Caterina instinctively shrinks away; the inclusive impulses of social workers irritate her. She hurries away and before leaving the building she sees some guards walking towards the bar without hearing the sound of their footsteps.

Since the doctor advised her not to put too much stress on her hip she cannot run or lift anything heavy any more, but she often goes for a walk along the Aniene.

That is where she found a dust-coloured cat one day; she picked it up, paying no attention to its protests and took it home with her so as not to feel so lonely.

The cat sleeps on her bed, occasionally, but spends most of the time with its head stuck between the railings on the balcony until Caterina's mother goes and rescues it. Every so often, when they stroke under its collar they find flakes of rust and paint.

On the river banks that she walks along, the grass is high and soft and her gym shoes leave light indistinct footprints that make her path indiscernible.

Caterina walks swiftly but now and again she stops to catch her breath and to press her aching hip, brushing aside the insects crawling on her neck while the light sets the river ablaze.

She passes the aluminium container cabins that have sprung up among the trees and which flooding will sooner or later turn into rafts, and she sees t-shirts hung up among the big fleshy leaves and hears someone laughing while trying to start an engine; the rubber cables that carry electricity to an amphibious population few Romans suspect the existence of, swing in the wind.

Caterina has never managed to set eyes on any of these people – sometimes she thinks she has only imagined them – but the coded signs of their presence comfort her because she feels close to a kind of religion of renunciation, whereby all that's necessary in order to live has been negotiated and then abandoned among plants and animals that are not listed among the protected species, yet they exist.

She continues walking until the muddy grass and the bushes become sparser and begin to give way to tarmac, then she keeps to the side of the road to avoid being hit by the cars that speed past her on Via Pietralata and exchange radiophonic interference at the traffic lights.

The policeman has invited her to supper and despite the distance she decides she will get to his place on foot. Caterina walks the kilometres separating her from Torpignattara until her calf muscles are aching and the effort makes her stumble;

on the stretches of road with no provision for pedestrians she flattens herself against the walls that are reduced to spongy barriers of volcanic tuff and passes the bus depots with dazed determination, in the rarefied haze of the traffic.

"You're all sweaty," says the policeman when he opens the door with a tea towel over his shoulder that Caterina finds sweet and ridiculous.

"I walked here," she replies, gasping.

"From where?"

"Rebibbia," she confesses before collapsing on the sofa.

"You're crazy."

Caterina is not listening, she takes off her shoes and falls asleep in the foetal position, engulfed by tiredness.

She wakes up half an hour later when she hears the sound of the shower and of bins being overturned; the light from the street lamps filtering in from the window becomes murkier and more nebulous.

She goes over to see what is happening and then shouts for the policeman to come; he joins her, leaving wet footprints on the floor.

"What is it?" asks the policeman, looking out of the window.

Caterina points a finger at the piles of rubbish and broken bottles on the other side of the road, where a group of protesters are overturning street bins.

"It must be a demonstration about that association they've closed down."

The policeman puts a hand on her hips and asks her if she wants to freshen up, Caterina shakes her head and breathes in the smell of burnt paper coming from the bins.

"Do you know why they did that?" she asks the policeman who has not stirred and is continuing to watch what is happening in the street.

"If they don't stop I'll have to go down," he says half-heartedly, and without moving away from the window. "No, I don't," he adds, before giving a whistle when a guy smashes a bottle against a car parked in front of the building opposite, but no one hears it.

"And it doesn't interest you? After all, you live here."

"Don't remind me," he says before slamming the window shut and going over to the sink.

"How do I clean this?" he asks Caterina, lifting up a shiny slippery sea bass.

"Cut it down the middle."

Caterina observes the policeman's fumbling motions, then tells him to step aside; he puts arms around her, holding her hips, while she scales the fish under running water.

"When I worked at the fishmonger's my fingers used to turn purple because of the ice, they only got back to normal hours later. Sometimes I was afraid they'd fall off. I always got up at six in the morning, I was a zombie," she tells him, shaking her head, immediately regretting this confession – she knows there's no going back from tenderness.

After supper they stretch out on the sofa to watch a DVD, but they are both distracted.

The policeman complains about the smell of smoke in the apartment despite the closed windows and Caterina loses control of her breathing.

"What's wrong?" he asks, caressing her stomach and lowering the volume.

"I don't know," replies Caterina, lying back limply.

The policeman detaches his gaze from the screen and stands up to give her more room; he makes her stretch out her legs and then presses two fingers to her jugular to measure her pulse before lifting her wrists above her head.

"Don't worry, I've done a first aid course," he tells her, smiling when she widens her eyes in the grip of confusion.

"I can't breathe properly."

"You're hyperventilating," says the policeman to calm her, but Caterina is frightened by the cold and remote tone of his voice, the one he uses to help lunatics and misfits on the street.

"I've never had a panic attack," she sobs before fainting.

The air is filled with the sound of sirens and ambulances and outside the window the smoke that comes from the rubbish bins continues to rise.

6

In the hotel every so often I watch television with the guests; we have a screen mounted in a corner of the foyer, but whenever I call it that the boss starts laughing.

"That's right, *the foyer*. You've no idea how much I had to pay to get it registered as a hotel and not a guest house."

Actually, seeing it from the entrance, the hotel where I work is not very different from the three-star places Aurelio and I booked when we went on holiday before we had enough money to rent the apartments with whirlpool baths.

Close to the reception desk there are two armchairs and a couple of chairs with brass trimmings that the cleaning ladies manage to put a shine on. With the glass-topped tables covered with magazines for which the subscription has not been renewed after the initial promotional offer, it looks almost like a dentist's waiting room. But there is nothing respectable about this hotel and no one stands on ceremony.

I always leave the television on during the night shift, even though I often can't hear anything because the security guard stationed at the front entrance wants to talk about referees being corrupt. I am happy to listen to him but with my eyes glued to the screen so he doesn't get any wrong ideas. He's married, but that doesn't mean anything.

The guard is a measure that was taken after two men came in wanting somewhere to sleep without having to pay and collapsed into the armchairs after splattering the floor with a stubbornly glutinous vomit the cleaners had to spend ages scrubbing to get off.

The owner was not worried but he is a family man and he looks out for me.

I have a suspicion the guard is here for other reasons too and I cannot understand where the money to pay him comes from. When I raise the subject he looks at me with a serious expression and says his salary is the fruit of "co-operation", and asks whether I understand what he means.

I respond vaguely, thinking perhaps he is talking about a co-operative, and anyway with the life I lead I don't want to go into it.

The nicest clients are the South American gentlemen who have a sister who's just become a nun and they can't stay in the convent because they've brought along too many nephews and nieces to visit the city. I don't know how they end up here, the hotel has only recently been on the internet and we get mostly telephone bookings; most people arrive at the last minute, passing by in their car.

Often they're clients from a nearby strip bar: I recognise them by their frustration, and because for a while I used to hang out with those types.

The hotel is located in a convenient and ambiguous position; it is close to all the betting halls that have been bought up by the Arabs and to the consultancy companies that are being promoted as a technology park.

The other clients I have a soft spot for are the engineers who come from some town in the north and as soon as they enter the hotel say there must have been some mistake, then they get on the phone and harangue a secretary who has booked a room by consulting Google Maps.

Basically, this area is full of offices.

I often manage to calm them down, and in the evening when they are bored they come and keep me company at the desk, along with the South American gentlemen who can't sleep because of jet lag.

The most overbearing ones want to change the television channel, but here the majority decides.

Sometimes these dissatisfied engineers trek off down the Tiburtina to buy a few tubs of ice-cream and we end up sitting there with the doors and windows open, the guard smiling at us and the hum of the fan in a corner – every so often we smell an insect getting fried in a lamp that's all blue and silver.

One evening I'm channel-hopping and I come across a report on evictions from occupied municipal buildings.

The images are blurry and all you can see are people crouched beneath plastic shields; one of the refugees is bleeding and for a second I think I recognise the policeman's union friend, but the camera shot breaks off and I don't have time to work out whether it really is him.

"These people!" says a woman who is falling asleep in her chair and I don't know whether she is talking about the police or the immigrants who have occupied the building.

One of the engineers asks me to change channel because there is live coverage of the poker championships in Monte Carlo, but I think he is just fed up with the violence.

"What kind of work were you doing before?" some clients ask, and that's my fault because as soon as we start chatting I explain I've only been here a little while and I won't be staying long, and they get curious.

Even the owner knows that when I am not busy deleting clients' names from the register I read the job advertisements.

"I was a dancer," I reply, and the clients laugh because it is not a real job.

Let alone when I say I was a stripper.

After the closure of the video rental store Aurelio and Marco borrowed some money and rented a small warehouse behind the television studios on the Tiburtina, formerly a medical supplies depot. After refurbishing, it looked like a garage fitted out by Russian engineers, but Mario liked it because the industrial look was fashionable.

They found some girls for the shows I was to choreograph, some had even studied dance abroad: it was my decision who we took on, then Mario started imposing his preferences and Aurelio stopped listening to me. Because of them, the dancers that turned up kept getting younger and less well trained, and when the takings began to drop Mario said we had to try something new.

The first time I stripped in public was not particularly memorable.

Even if they tell you to go slowly and to make it last as long as you can – the rule is to take as much time as possible before you are left without any clothes on – when you're on stage everything follows a different, almost extraterrestrial time-scale, and what with the music that stupefies you and the dim lighting you feel as if you are looking at the public through gauze.

With stag parties it was much simpler, generally they were all too drunk to realise what was going on and the awkwardness of some of the guys made me feel sorry for them – they were my age and about to get married and they had to take part in this farce to get a few photos to post. I could spot the ones that felt embarrassed straightaway and I helped them.

It wasn't the men I found physically unattractive that were the problem – I would try to make sure they were the ones I had to deal with, without Mario realising it – but those I wanted to be fondled by, the well-dressed ones who drank slowly. The strippers loved saying no one was allowed to kiss them, it made them feel more elegant and mysterious, but it was only the clients I found repulsive that I warned off.

There were some guys I even allowed to lick my teeth.

When one of those men kept putting banknotes on the table and asked you to stay a while longer even if the show was over, and you collapsed on top of him hiding his face in your hair, excited by your own sweat, his moan of satisfaction when he slipped a hand between your thighs and discovered you were wet, the grip on your arse tightening, more domineering, the mouth clamped to your breast and when it came away covered with glitter that you licked off and they tasted of fruity-flavoured glue – you liked it – when you looked at the other girls who adopted the most fluid and strangest positions, lying on tables, head down on the floor, clinging to a pole with their hands and with their ankles crossed; girls who laughed with strong accents and low-pitched voices, legs black from rubbing against the stage, costumes semi-abandoned on the floor, hair with kinks made by hairpins pulled out for clients, lace around their eyes, nipples with the adhesive from the shiny tassles left on them, cellulite that showed up only in a certain light, their bitchiness in the changing room, their comments about orgasms, hands sticky with sperm, the smell of self-tanning lotion, the spare pairs of tights in the drawers, the fake snakes for those who pretended to be dominatrixes, the names that had to be invented, the mobile numbers that were always being changed, the sexy languid syllables, the scents, the make-up with ridiculous names and the bruises, sometimes, when a client did not stop in time.

The company gave me money to buy costumes from the wholesale stores behind Termini station. We learned from experience that green wigs didn't suit anybody and only the really beautiful girls could wear the blue ones.

Not all the girls were happy to strip: once a dancer called Marta arrived early for rehearsal. While I was sweeping the floor of the dressing room she explained to me her theory about invisible drilling.

"It's like having a Black & Decker put to your stomach, someone presses the button and starts drilling, just a little every day. I don't feel the pain but I see the hole getting bigger.

She lifted up her top and placed both hands on her stomach as if showing me she was pregnant. "Soon I'll have a hole going right through me and no one will be able to see it," she said, popping a mint into her mouth.

I stripped in public and pretended to fuck clients until

Aurelio threw me against a wall shattering my hip and I couldn't dance any more.

My bones are big and weak but if I had been more careful about my diet perhaps they would not have broken like that.

The strippers were beautiful, young, with no scars. They took drugs, I didn't.

They didn't do it to make what happened bearable but to be more laid-back and better at it and to me it was like being back at school again, when I was the only one who didn't smoke in the loos.

After the accident I took on the job of make-up artist, everyone in the club knew I had been downgraded but the girls were kind and when they had skin problems or bruises I did my best to conceal them.

I would type Brigitte Bardot, Dita Von Teese or Cleopatra into Aurelio's computer to follow tutorials on how to do their make-up, then I would draw long black lines on the dancers' eyelids and made them look proud and gilded like an Egyptian goddess who came to power without renouncing love.

I bought heavy-duty foundation on the internet, the kind Thai dancers use that does not melt even at forty degrees. I had to use both hands to spread it on. When they looked at themselves in the mirror they would nod with satisfaction, sometimes they called me Photoshop, and left money for me at the end of their shift; I would put it aside to pay the bills and every time I went to the post office to make the payments I would feel better – still useful, human.

Putting make-up on a girl who has taken a lot of punishment is like putting make-up on a corpse, despite the layers of greasepaint the blemish always comes to the surface.

To clients, bruises were disturbing; a stripper could be fat but she must not have any marks or contusions.

That's why Mario would get angry with the ones that were too thin: in a nightclub you don't make money out of suffering or your past life. Sometimes I would take them home when they were evicted or didn't have anywhere to go; my mother would say I wasn't making friends but creating a colony of parasites. Once I even helped one of them to go cold turkey, I was with her while she sweated under my cartoon-patterned sheets, I made her broth and then I sent her back to her parents on a Wizz Air flight paid for by Aurelio. I sat at the foot of her bed and held her hand when she couldn't sleep – we couldn't keep the lights on because they hurt her eyes.

Someone told me they had seen her months later at a rave in Nettuno, she was standing in front of a tree semi-naked with her hair loose; she was talking about red horses and oceans in flames.

I don't have her number to ask her whether it's true and I'm sorry I lost it.

The club was shut down by the police a year after I stopped stripping but it had already been in decline for a while: our clients were ever older men and they didn't have to dress well to get in.

It was during that period that I met the policeman.

Generally after they had got their drinks the clients went into the performance room but the policeman remained sitting on a stool in front of his draught beer, ordering one drink after another while I apologised for how hot it was.

That nearness unnerved me; I have never been good at mixing cocktails or sugaring the rims of glasses.

I noticed he had strong shoulders and dark hair, but not quite dark enough to be black, of a thick spiky texture, as if it had grown back after being completely shaven.

(Aurelio says it doesn't grow back the same after a military cut, the structure of the hair changes: that's why he doesn't want to have his hair cut in prison.)

I was careful not to stare at him too much but when I took a twenty-euro banknote from him he stroked my palm absent-mindedly, I made a mistake working out the change and gave him back too much.

"If you want I'll keep it," he said, laughing when I apologised for the confusion, and it was at that point that I had to go out the back to get some air.

The policeman followed me out to smoke a cigarette and started asking questions, kicking a plastic cup that someone had used as an ashtray and spilling water and cigarette butts over the tarmac. I memorised it all – the lamp post with tyre shop stickers and the telephone numbers of lonely people on it, the rubbish bins and the liquefied lights of the night traffic – but I did not focus on him or on his face.

I gave him the telephone number when he asked me for it because things with Aurelio had been going badly since he slammed me against the wall.

The policeman did not pursue me much – it was always me that wrote first and the time he sent me a heart-shaped emoji I had to check the message a couple of times to be sure it was from him. Now I know that to a certain extent he used me for the investigation, but he likes me, although that's not saying much: the policeman doesn't have many friends, he had a brother who died, and he has bags under his eyes more miserable-looking than mine which he can't cover up with foundation.

My mother says I'm capable of causing lightbulbs to explode at a glance and of reversing the motion of the planets, although I've never wanted to have any superpowers and I'm not a natural disaster.

However, sometimes I do think I'm a hero, especially when I think how I reacted when I fractured my hip: I've never told anyone how it happened; I hate complaining and it's that strength that holds me together.

When my bones ache and my friends pity me for the men in my life who've ended up in prison; when the policeman deplores my situation and an acquaintance who lives in a better neighbourhood than mine is apologetic, I smile and nod but I avoid blaming anyone for my woes.

Blaming others makes me feel dirty and sticky like when you come out of the gym without having had a shower and you have to travel on the bus and your hair won't tuck behind your ears properly and everyone is pretending they can't smell your body odour when even you yourself find it intolerable and you're ashamed.

The hotel guests and the cleaning ladies who now know my story by heart – these days I don't have many friends I can talk to – ask me whether I don't feel guilty about having a clandestine relationship and I try to explain that actually it is like having two hearts, not just one, and that I don't feel I'm betraying Aurelio but simply boosting my blood circulation and becoming stronger, like a vampire that instead of biting into someone's neck falls in love.

Their eyes widen as I speak but it's clear they are amused and perhaps even envious.

I always answer the questions they ask about sex because I'm not ashamed of those any more – the way in which the policeman holds my hands above my head and makes me convulse as if he had attached me to a defibrillator, or when we make love without looking at each other and I find myself with bits of hair and pillow in my mouth and I think I might suffocate – but I know this situation is coming to an end. And I don't know how to put into words the sadness I feel.

Sometimes the cleaning ladies tell me that despite everything I'm a good kid, sex is healthy and I deserve every kind of consolation, then they confess to having a daughter or a granddaughter who wants to be a dancer. To put their minds at rest I explain that nothing special is needed. Anyone can acquire muscles that don't tremble even under the most intense strain: the bundle of skin and nerves you turn into after years of practice, and in the long run make you look ugly, is not proof of any particular talent, just perseverance.

They nod and we spend the rest of our waking hours continuing to chat to the *basso continuo* of the television, comparing the side effects and advantages of contraceptives.

7

"When the doors open, evacuate the carriage. When the doors open, evacuate the carriage. We ask passengers to remain calm as they leave."

The train driver's voice breaks off and the subway carriage remains dark. When the doors open with a rasping ferric exhalation, people start pushing Caterina towards the doors, ignoring the calls for order.

It is the beginning of September, people don't smell of sunscreen any more and there are fewer foreigners to be heard, although Caterina hears one passenger who has got out of the carriage saying something in German strongly punctuated with question marks – no one is able to answer him.

Beneath the glare of the emergency spotlights, the Line B tunnel takes on an almost hallowed look.

Caterina does not offer any resistance to the flow around her and allows herself to be carried along by the passengers whose fear and motivation are greater than hers. One woman says: "It had to happen tonight," referring to the all-night culture fest going on, while some people mispronounce the name of the terrorist groups they assume are involved. Others worry about the frozen meat that will have to be thrown out.

Stopping on the platform, Caterina wonders whether her friends who have taken the bus will manage to get home and she takes her mobile from her bag, despite knowing there is no signal down there.

She has not spoken to Aurelio for a week because of a row in circumstances that have already become hazy: it is the first time they have taken such a long break from each other but now Caterina would like to call him to find out where he is while the city is swallowed up in darkness and the most ignorant people around her are convinced they are now in a state of war, as he called it the day the regional news bulletin broadcast the information that someone had fired gunshots in the McDonald's they always go to.

Caterina manages to move close to the mouth of the tunnel where she can lean her back against the wall and separate herself from the others: some passengers form an unintentional procession to reach the entrance gates. She waits to find out whether it is a temporary failure, she doesn't know how she will get home otherwise.

She wipes from her forehead a drop of condensation from the ceiling; when the smell from the worn brakes subsides, Caterina notices a more organic earthy smell. It is almost nauseating but she can't stop inhaling it. Despite the clamour and complaints of anxious people, down there it seems to her all mysterious and feral, then she comes back out because there is an announcement no more trains will be arriving and the city has turned into a hospital ward where old people coming out of the museums – admission being free today – grope their way along the walls and can't make telephone calls.

Waiting at the traffic lights by the Circo Massimo valley, Caterina considers the idea of hitchhiking. She looks at the front seats of the cars around her: she sees one man beating his head repeatedly against the car horn; a girl in the passenger seat gazes at her with commiseration, proud of the illuminated metal cage that isolates her from the chaos in the streets.

This is not the first time she has been trapped underground: in middle school during a visit to the catacombs, ignoring the warning the guide had given, urging the students to stay in pairs, she had stopped to tie the laces of her gym shoes.

Before she stood up again she had wasted time examining a pebble that looked like a tooth, then put it in her pocket, and when she looked round everyone had disappeared. She was not scared, but instead of staying where she was and waiting for someone to come back to fetch her, she went on, venturing down passages that became ever lower and narrower. Only when she felt she was hallucinating from staring at the symmetrical holes in the stone did she begin to scream.

When they got to her, the teachers asked what she thought she was doing, while her classmates made fun of her; she was too relieved to care.

That evening she showed the pebble to her parents and they decided to put it in a glass jar with the date on it and the various possible provenances.

Her father had written the words *Lion? Emperor? Jewish prisoner?* in tiny wavery handwriting and for a while they had treated it like a relic.

Undecided whether to cross at the junction or to remain near the station and wait until power is restored, Caterina just keeps standing at the traffic lights while the faces and stances of the people around her changed.

The incident in the catacombs had no psychological consequences but according to her mother it brought back her rheumatism. As a child she had suffered inexplicable aches in her bones, she would always wake up round about three in the morning and go crying to her parents' room, where she would lie between them complaining of intense, constant, throbbing pain.

Her father would rub her shoulders to no effect because the pain was internal, and he would sing her lullabies; her mother would be dismissive, telling her in a sleepy voice it was just growing pains. They went to a rheumatologist to solve the problem, then the doctor asked about the heating at home and the possible presence of mould. Her parents took offence but were rude about the doctor only after they had got back to the car.

Caterina has to go across because a girl bumps into her with her elbow and pushes her into the road; after a little uncertainty she decides to sit on the grass in the Circo Massimo and wait for the sun to rise. She settles herself near a group surrounded by empty glass bottles and paper napkins, then she gets out the sweatshirt she has put in her bag and spreads it out on the grass to protect her legs from the damp.

She checks the time on her phone, it is a couple of hours until dawn and the end of the blackout.

A guy crouched down by a citronella candle gets up and comes over to Caterina to ask her for a light, but she does not smoke.

"Have you visited any museums?" he asks after gazing at her intently.

"No, my friends wanted to do some shopping. We went to Via del Corso."

"You can do that all year," the guy says with a crooked smile; Caterina shrugs her shoulders and looks down at her phone which has just lit up. It is only her mother.

"Not answering, eh?" he asks, sitting down beside her when he sees her dispirited expression.

The guy has crusty eyes. Caterina thinks maybe he spent the summer in Africa, in one of those villages where mammals are mauled to death in the sun, staining the ground with purple blood, and he has come back with some illness without realising it.

He opens a beer with his key ring, drinks some and then offers a sip to Caterina who puts her lips to the neck of the bottle without wiping it.

"I've got a boyfriend," she says when he gets too close to her shoulder.

"And what's the problem?" he answers without losing his composure.

"We've had a row."

"And why's that?"

"He says I've changed."

"Everyone changes," he says with a grimace that makes her want to be kissed.

"He doesn't like my friends; he says they make me feel frustrated."

"He's jealous, he'll get over it."

Caterina nods, and places the palms of her hands on the ground behind her, leaning back as if she were on the beach.

"Are you in love?"

"My mother says it's a mistake. I'm too young to get tied down," she replies, observing the park area crowded with people; a few metres away a woman is sleeping with her arms around her dog.

Caterina looks up and gazes at the stars pulsing at irregular intervals, then puts the bottle to her ear and inclines her head to hear the sound the wind makes inside it.

The sound reminds her of her mother's breath in her ear whenever she had a high temperature and her mother would try to calm her, murmuring incoherent words.

"Well, good luck," says the guy, taking the bottle of beer from her hand and hurling it to the bottom of the dip – this time the glass doesn't make any sound. Then he gets up with a synchronised movement of his arms and legs and walks away without inviting her to join his group.

Caterina checks her mobile again, her friends have not texted to ask if she is all right. Actually she doesn't have many friends, just people who have known her for years.

After her father's arrest, her grades went down and she left school; now she hands out newspapers outside Tiburtina station and often goes out with the other girls doing the same job.

Almost all of them are enrolled at university and some of them live in the student hall of residence at Casal Bertone. When they are working they wear coloured waterproof jackets like those of petrol station attendants, as protection against the occasional shower and to make the passengers, who can help them get rid of their pile of newspapers, feel sorry for them.

Caterina recognises the commuters – some of them always smile at her – and her days are punctuated by the same rituals: the complaints about pay from the guys who deliver the papers, the bets on how long the new recruits will last, the litany from the woman who berates her because instead of the newspaper she wants fliers with supermarket discount vouchers.

Sometimes she has to leave home at five and gets on the bus with the cleaning ladies and the street vendors – her dawns are imbued with spices and aggressive male deodorants.

Every day she sees the sign *LORDS OF TIBURTOWN* on a building alongside the platforms; she knows it is a reference to an American film about skateboarding but she has never come across anyone with a skateboard outside the station – perhaps there aren't enough humps and dips.

Caterina likes it because it seems familiar, as if it belonged to a band.

She too once had something written on a wall for her.

A week after she and Aurelio became officially engaged, he took her to an open space behind a supermarket and showed her a graffito of her name on the tarmac – a crude yellow sign with spaced lettering, the same colour combination as on hazard signs for radioactive material. Caterina smiled and told him he was mad but she knew it had been there long before she and Aurelio met each other.

She has never confessed this so as not to make him feel bad: the people you love have to be protected.

This is something she has known since going to visit her father in prison; in the visiting room what's more important is what you don't say to each other. It's the language she has learnt at Rebibbia, similar to the one real criminals use when they have to pass information to the outside so as not to lose control over their affairs: the things and the feelings they talk about turn into a constellation of opposites and contraries.

Aurelio doesn't like her job at the station but Caterina is afraid to give it up and stay at home doing nothing again; every time he suggests finding something different she resists.

When he is busy in the evening with kickboxing workouts Caterina goes with her co-workers to a bar in the Casal Bertone neighbourhood where they often get a discount or free drinks. The owners have put a palm tree covered with red lights at the entrance to attract customers but it makes it look like a sex shop.

(Aurelio and Marco are still intending to open a nightclub one day; she thinks they ought to be careful with that colour.)

Every so often one of her girlfriends drinks too much and starts saying, "Hey, she's a dancer," pointing a finger at Caterina in an attempt to attract the interest of the men playing on the slot machine by the door. Tall men, generally married, their hair thick with gel.

She hopes they find her attractive and she blushes.

Her muscles slack with tiredness, Caterina tries to extend the damp sweatshirt so she can stretch out better while the sky starts to crack like an eggshell – translucid yellow leaking into an otherwise still grey mass as light as a bird's feather.

"What's so special about it?" Aurelio asks her when he gets suspicious because she is spending so much time in that student hall of residence.

"It's fun, different things happen every evening."

She tells him about the card games in the kitchen and the meals where they exchange recipes from their country of origin, but not about the ambulances that come at regular intervals for students having panic attacks, the guards in the security booth at the entrance who don't ask for your identity card to let you in if you stop and listen to their jokes, or about the booze stolen from supermarkets.

Being part of these gatherings is fun but unlike her friends Caterina never has to sit university exams and so sometimes she feels a bit lonely and out of place when they are studying, yet she stays sitting on their balcony overlooking a drug addicts' rehabilitation centre, seeing only German Shepherd dogs going in there.

While the girls make notes and revise quietly, stubbing out their cigarettes in empty coconut shells, she plaits her hair in the afternoon sun as warm as a telephone token rubbed for too long; but when they leave to go back to their home country or to go on holiday Caterina finds herself wandering through a quiet and redundant neighbourhood, hating the sound of rubber balls bounced against a wall and the lethargy of the greengrocers' open at three in the afternoon.

Caterina waits until the sun has completely risen and beneath the misty light she walks back to the subway entrance – the trains have started running again.

She comes out at Pietraltra station and there is almost no trace of the blackout: the cardboard boxes full of goods to be sorted, the cacophony of mothers shouting at their children to wake up, the barking of dogs – all the mundanities of daily life spewed up from the darkness.

She enters the apartment, listening out for any sound, but

anything. After a few months it grows back just as it was before.

"Yes. I've had enough, you've no idea what kind of people are out on the streets at night."

"Did I tell you I saw one of your colleagues on television?"

"No," says the policeman with slight interest.

"He was doing an eviction; it was when you cleared out a reception centre for refugees."

"But that was months ago."

"Once in the hotel I caught a documentary about the indigenous people of the Amazon forest who were coming into contact with outsiders for the very first time. Your friend had exactly the same look on his face," says Caterina.

"In what way?"

"He didn't even recognise the people in front of him as human beings."

"You know nothing," the policeman says in a resentful tone. "In one occupied building we found children with scabies and polio; there are diseases in those places that weren't around even at the time of the colonial campaigns in Africa. Not even when my grandfather was in the war. What were we supposed to do, leave them there?" he asks before getting up to fetch something from the desk.

"A boy in the reception centre at Tor Tre Teste jumped off the building as soon as we got there," he continues without raising the tone of his voice. "He threw himself from the second floor, then realised he was still alive and crawled over to a colleague, asking to be shot. You've no idea how many people want to die."

"You're saying they're asking for it," says Caterina.

"No, but if you kill them sometimes you're doing them a favour," he replies before throwing a sealed envelope on to her bare stomach. Caterina opens it and finds two tickets for a dance show with a birthday card.

"Take your mother. Or your boyfriend."

"How do you know it's my birthday?" she asks, ignoring that comment.

"I photocopied your identity card at the station when you made a statement, remember?"

Caterina pulls the sheet over her face.

"It's the most romantic thing you've ever done for me," she murmurs through a layer of fabric that in the thirty-four degree heat barely mitigated by the air conditioner is like a sweat-inducing shroud.

"Sorry if I snapped at you. I didn't sleep last night," says the policeman without coming back to bed.

"Neither did I, it must be the weather."

When she leaves the building Caterina feels the oppression of a city where the breaths of wind feel like spiders crawling over your skin and the humidity collects in tears.

She walks towards the bus stop, then the policeman calls to her from the window.

"Hey!" he says with a timid smile, his hands resting on the windowsill, his muscles tensed under his short-sleeved t-shirt, and Caterina stands there with her forearm resting on her forehead, protecting herself against the sun. "Come back soon," says the policeman but a scooter going by at that moment drowns out her reply.

12

I was born after an eight-hour operation that almost killed my mother.

My father gave her a venereal disease during her pregnancy, a nasty and shameful infection which the nurses talked about in the corridors, pitying her. The doctors on the other hand were excited because they could save someone's life in a new way.

That's what my mother says: the doctors hovered around her, their eyes feverish and glistening, frightening her. But they were honest with her: they explained it might be better to remove the foetus and forgo having a daughter. That either she would die, or I would die, or we would both die.

My mother gave her permission for the operation signing her name in pen on sheets of paper, and sometimes I think the whole of her life has been spent in the fear and resignation of that signature.

It's just that I have a will of my own and I was born. When

I told this story to Aurelio to make him fall in love with me, he said he was overwhelmed with tenderness.

The evening of my thirty-first birthday Aurelio takes me out to dinner. At first I think he wants to only because he has found a restaurant where they serve pizza with a topping of some citrus fruit I've never heard of. I know he cooked a lot in Rebibbia but since he's been out that habit has become an obsession – his brother told me he wastes hours in the supermarket deciding which olive oil to buy; he is looking for the greenest and the purest.

"Better to be like this than feeling depressed," he said, and I have to agree with him.

When we are seated in front of each other I try to look at Aurelio as if he were someone I didn't know. The restaurant dining rooms look like the ones in the farmhouses in the Zorro TV series, with terracotta-coloured walls and pictures full of pomegranates – before I met the policeman I might have thought it was elegant.

The candle on our table goes out twice; when the waiter comes over to take our order and relight it, Aurelio waves his hand to indicate that it doesn't matter, we can do without.

Aurelio smiles, leaning back in his chair, and tapping the table with his knife, I grab his hand because the sound of the metal on the tablecloth irritates me.

"There, stay still."

"How are you?" I ask immediately afterwards.

"It's odd. When it's my birthday nothing happens but when it's yours I feel older," he replies ignoring my question and starting to fiddle with the knife again after freeing his hand.

"It's becoming impossible to talk to you," I tell him.

"What do you want me to say? I don't think about it that much but I do still think about it. Prison is like a pantomime… there's the mad, the bad and the ugly. There's the fag, there's the guard. In fact, the guards are probably even worse, because someone like me gets out at least. You try being in there day after day. Some of them are bastards," he says "bastards" like one of those workers who chain themselves to the gates on the regional news on television, with the same slightly desperate and ridiculous emphasis, "but there's the odd one you can't help liking. He's a prisoner just like you, after all."

"That's not what I was asking, I want to know how you are now."

I lean towards him, irritated by the arrival of the waiter bringing our order.

"It's the mould," says Aurelio. "The worst thing is the mould on the walls and in the corners. It makes you feel like an animal in a pen. You feel that hairy green stuff attacking your lungs. I want to check the figures, I think everyone who's been in Rebibbia ends up dead within twenty years."

Some time ago I went with him to collect the results of some blood test – he had them done in a private clinic to speed things up. The assistant took a while to track them down, and Aurelio was sat there on the chair beside me, fidgeting, suddenly jumping up every now and again.

"Did something happen to you in prison?" I found the courage to ask him – perhaps that was the reason he was getting the blood tests and he didn't know how to tell me.

"No," he replied, clenching his teeth, offended.

"Then there's this thing about work. Partly it's rehabilitation but at the same time they're exploiting you. You're in prison making things and then someone sells them. And who do almost all the profits go to?" he asks.

"It's better than having nothing to do," I say, cutting the crusts off the pizza; Aurelio puts them in his mouth without saying anything.

When he checked the results in the car he said they were good, the readings for his liver were actually closer to normal. He seemed upset by this, as if his body had improved in prison.

His brother told me that at meal times Aurelio sometimes seems paranoid, he gets bogged down in political rants that make his parents feel uncomfortable because they don't know how to respond – every time they hear talk about rights they get nervous and think they've done something wrong.

His mother tries to fill his glass with wine, hoping he will soon feel sleepy and go off to bed quietly, but Aurelio doesn't drink now.

"Once Tony called me, you remember him?" he says, having asked the waiter for the menu again. I don't know what happens to all the food he puts away, his features are so sharp and defined, but perhaps he'll be able to eat as much as he wants from now on – his body will always have to compensate.

Tony is a prosecco sales rep, gay, married and short, who supplies the Lazio area for an agency in Trieste. Whenever he came to talk to Aurelio and Marco he used to say he couldn't stay long because he had other business customers to visit but he never managed to get away without having opened at least one sample bottle. When I came in to do my shift I'd find them in the office with sweaty hair, choking with laughter over some stupid private joke.

"Of course, any man who wears shirts like that is impossible to forget."

"He called to tell me he'd been in prison as well. Six months in Belgium, before he came to Italy. That was unexpected."

"What for?"

"What?"

"What did he end up in prison for?"

Aurelio shook his head, disappointed.

"I don't know, I didn't ask. It wasn't important," he says, falling silent, but I need to hear him speak, so I ask him questions about his cellmates' families, and he tells me stories – amusing, sad, desperate stories – about escapes, suicides, hunger strikes, letters, divorces, distant lands.

"You met all those people," I say in an almost nostalgic tone as he pays the bill.

"I wasn't at some party."

"Sometimes, in the hotel, I meet interesting people and I think I'm like you, that I know how to talk to them. How to do it in such a way they remember having met me. But you're better at it than I am, nothing disgusts you."

"That's not true: mould disgusts me, Turkish baths disgust me, dirty teeth disgust me. But people don't disgust me. After all sooner or later everybody makes mistakes; we're all the same," he says, putting his credit card back in his wallet. Then he bursts out laughing at himself. "I talk like the Pope, my mother's right."

"Perhaps the Buddhist manual has driven you insane."

"But I'm surviving," he says, looking me in the eye and throwing some small change on the table as a tip.

When we come out of the restaurant we pass close to some

plane trees with big crooked roots that have broken through the tarmac; the lights in people's houses have gone out and the absence of voices around us is unnerving.

"I'll take you home, you're working tomorrow," Aurelio decides, but I ask him if we can carry on in the car for a bit. Only after a while do I realise we are going in the direction of the nightclub.

Behind the Tiburtina television studios are some semi-residential buildings with space left between them for sheds and warehouses and for gardens full of dog kennels made of wood and mismatched bricks.

When we went to view the premises for the first time, Mario thought it was ideal: it was somewhere close and inaccessible, you could pass in front of it countless times and still not notice it.

But just next door there were places with people living in them, one-storey houses with gardens; the inhabitants were women who in summer would bring out Coca-Cola beach umbrellas and lie stretched out on wooden sun-beds as if they were on holiday, remembering every now and again to water palm trees with ragged trunks and dry leaves the colour of sand.

They never greeted us and when they went off to visit their children I did not miss them.

Aurelio parked the car in front of the nightclub's lowered shutters; the police tape indicating the area had been cordoned off, was torn and lay coiled on the street.

Under the street lights the place was the same dull pink of the sky after fireworks have been let off; it seemed almost romantic.

"I shouldn't have involved you, I wasn't in my right mind. It's the thing I regret most," says Aurelio after a while.

"For a while I liked it. I can fend for myself," I replied, lowering the window to release the overpowering smell of the perfume I had just sprayed on my wrists, the same one I used to sprinkle on the letters I wrote to him when he was in prison.

"I know."

"I've been fending for myself ever since I was born. It's a genetic thing, I'll pass it on to my kids. Think carefully before you marry me," I say, hoping to make him laugh.

"I don't know whether I want to get married," Aurelio replies. His voice is controlled, steady. Instead of looking at me he stares at the emblem at the centre of the steering wheel.

"Nor do I," I reply, a little confused, without knowing whether it is true or not.

"You know how to get by, you've even moved into a place of your own. But I don't know what to do, it's something I have to work out for myself."

"But you got through Rebibbia by yourself."

"I don't even know whether I want to have sex any more."

"What's that got to do with it?"

"It's something you should know," he says, running a hand over the back of his neck to loosen the contracted muscles.

"You're going to be a priest?" I say with a demented bitter laugh, before realising I am sitting beside a person who isn't suffering any more.

Aurelio now feels special because of the mould, the one hour outside in the open air, the boredom, the confinement.

"Look at me," I tell him, even though we are in the dark.

"I don't know whether I can be the same as before. You

were right," he replies continuing to stare at the wheel.

As a child I believed in the existence of the time machine, but that it could not be marketed because it was reserved for qualified people like astronauts.

For me it was something real, like the landing of a man on the moon, a mixture of magic and television.

I had come across it in a comic strip in which the protagonists travel from pre-history to a hyper-galactic future that was all black, chrome steel and stars, and afterwards I looked up Einstein in an illustrated encyclopedia for children.

At school they thought I was stupid because I kept drawing black holes and prototypes of time machines that travelled through them. Basically I was a mechanic's daughter and I liked circuitry but it became an obsession and when I realised this machine did not exist – not even in a bunker in America or in some secret space station run by NASA – I was plunged into a persistent and lonely depression, and incapable of sharing my disappointment.

However, my father understood and he took me to see *Jurassic Park* to help me get over it.

"Let's go and eat watermelon," I say to Aurelio.

"At this hour?" he asks, his eyes widening after lighting up the face of his watch to show me how late it is.

"You haven't given me a birthday present."

"I paid for the meal."

I look at Aurelio the way I do when I want something, with my mouth shut tight and my dimple showing.

Once we get to the melon stall, we sit next to a couple of teenagers who are counting the seeds, having spat them out, and are competing with each other for who has the most.

I'm not hungry but the lights of the metal booth and the music from the loudspeaker make me want to dance. I am about to ask Aurelio what he thinks of this song that has become a recent hit, then I realise he may not know it and that's something else we've lost out on over the past year, and so I say nothing.

Aurelio looks up and says perhaps he should go out more in the evening, I nod, fixing my gaze on the flower stall right next to us – a man parks suddenly, to buy last-minute flowers.

I am touched when I see men buying roses at two in the morning: I think of the women they are seeing, the mothers they are going to visit in hospital, the vases these women immediately go looking for to save themselves from the embarrassment this kindness gives rise to.

I must have a glazed look in my eyes because Aurelio leaps up and goes over to the flower stall, then comes back to me with a bunch of yellow fleshy dahlias.

"It's her birthday," he tells the lads who congratulate him on his purchase, I suck the fruit juice from my fingers and take the plastic wrapping off the flowers to count them.

"An uneven number, that's a good sign," I say, sniffing the flower heads.

"I missed this," says Aurelio, and I don't know whether he's talking about summer evenings, what you learn about life from street vendors, or even just this smell, which is a mixture of wet grass and rubber dinghies, hair spray and dried fruit. I watch the lads who are ordering more to eat. Even though they don't look like Aurelio when he was their age, there is something familiar about their happy shining eyes and their tanned calves made smooth by the exhaust silencers on their scooters.

"If we could travel back in time, where would you go?" I ask him.

"We can't."

"The night that Roma won the championship," says one of the lads although no one asked him.

"You weren't even born," remonstrates the stall keeper before coming over to clean the melon seeds off the table.

"But if we could?" I insist.

"OK. The year we opened the video rental store. It was fun," replies Aurelio.

"That doesn't count."

"Or the time we spent doing up the nightclub."

"You're only talking about work, that's sad. Try again."

"When we went to Mexico and got hit by typhoons," he says after a bit of thought.

It was a fun and disastrous holiday that Aurelio paid for; it was too hot to wear anything but we slept in each other's arms all the same. The house was full of scorpions but after a few days we stopped complaining about them; we even deluded ourselves we could distinguish the various species. My skin got so tanned it seemed to Aurelio as if he was making love to someone else.

One evening we were careless and he came inside me but instead of worrying about it we just lay there staring at the ceiling, holding hands and fantasising about not going back, joking about names for a baby the way people do when they are not afraid of anything.

"It rained the whole time," I say, wrapping up the flowers again so they wouldn't get spoiled.

"I don't know what the right answer is," he says and I see

a lost, almost dazed look on his face, so I take his hand and drop the subject.

"I don't much feel like going to sleep," I confess when we get back in the car but this time Aurelio does not listen to me.

We drive for a few kilometres in silence, illuminated by the phosphorescent lights of the banks and supermarkets on either side of the road, then he suddenly brakes and I instinctively grab the dashboard, without feeling alarmed.

"Sorry," he says, turning off the engine and pointing to the moon, flat and close up to us, that seems to be bursting through the bonnet.

"Are you sure we can park here?" I ask without taking my eyes off the planetary satellite.

"The worst they can do is arrest me," Aurelio says jokingly.

I turn and for the first time since he has come out of prison I see a gummy smile with too much mouth showing.

13

Caterina finds a bridal gown in a shop not far from where she lives with a display of blown-up photos of famous actresses dressed in white pinned to the drapes in the window.

The sun shining on the window has faded the smiles of the models and the once-pink lips have turned grey – they look like brides enrolled in a cryonics programme.

Her mother persuades her to go in to make fun of the antiquated models but the shop owner is shrewd and experienced, and Caterina finds herself with her arms wrapped in lengths of shiny satin. On some fabric samples green mould spores are discernible.

Caterina puts the fabrics down on a stool and strokes a dress covered with rhinestones without suppressing a grimace.

"Don't say anything until you've seen it on," the woman urges her, drawing back the curtains of a fitting room full of boxes with labels displaying flesh-coloured reinforced bras.

Caterina puts on the dress and emerges from the cubicle

to get a better look at herself in the mirror. Her mother does not cry, she just says, "Crazy that such an ugly dress should suit you so well."

The shop owner is busy fixing the flounces under the skirt for her, and even if she has heard she does not appear to take offence. Caterina strokes the openwork fabric over her bust and then sneezes repeatedly; the woman gets to her feet and exclaims, "There we are. What did I tell you? And don't worry about the dust, one wash and it will all come out."

While she is behind the curtains getting dressed again, the owner, proud of her infallible business instinct, asks, "When's the wedding?" Caterina hears her mother declare some date at random, then they solemnly walk out of the shop, and explode with laughter only after they have gone round the corner.

One day, perhaps, Caterina will buy that dress.

She has not seen the policeman for weeks, but having gathered further information about Aurelio's case and the closure of the nightclub, he goes to the hotel to see her.

Caterina does not want to talk to him in reception – the frosted glass windows make the lighting dingy – so she leaves a note on the counter telling any unlikely client she will be back soon. She takes him by the hand and leads him to the floor above; she has decided to change the sheets in a room that does not need cleaning.

"You won't believe it," says the policeman plonking himself down on the bed and removing his jacket.

Not wanting to make too much of this gesture, Caterina takes a pair of sheets from the cupboard and unfolds them with a firm shake, whipping the air.

"Guess who framed your boyfriend."

Caterina adopts a strange expression and immediately thinks of her father.

"Are you going to faint? Here I am to revive you again," the policeman teases her, and at that moment she feels a stab of pain in her chest, thinking how close they were during the early months of the summer.

"One of the dancers. She was the one who said there was drug-dealing and prostitution going on in the nightclub, one of my colleagues has confirmed it. She called us a few weeks ago to ask if she could give another statement. She told us the strippers were stealing money from Aurelio and Marco; they had made an agreement with people they knew to blackmail them and share the proceeds. At first we just laughed."

Caterina flops down beside him then straightens up as soon as she catches sight of her reflection in the mirror; her hair is full of static and fuzzy. She starts slowly disentangling it to make it smoother, she still wants him to think she's attractive.

"But then we checked out their bank transactions. They paid the money in a little at a time but there was still too much of it. When Aurelio told me someone was blackmailing him I thought he was crazy," the policeman goes on, not allowing himself to be distracted by Caterina's hypnotic movements.

"Why did the person who filed the complaint not tell you before? I can't understand it."

Last autumn, when the dancer with the scorpion tattoo came back after her convalescence, she followed a client into a private booth to offer him an exclusive performance; the man was an off-duty police officer and he was with a group celebrating a stag night. After her breast operation the dancer had found the striptease routine challenging and when she returned to work she had been taking more painkillers than necessary, putting in performances in a state of semi-consciousness. In the private booth the policeman, disappointed and embarrassed by the girl wriggling about on top of him, wiped her forehead with a wet handkerchief soaked in champagne, and stroked her back, trying to calm her sobs. The dancer told him there was cocaine circulating in the nightclub, that she was fed up with taking drugs, and when she asked for a pay rise one of the owners had suggested she prostitute herself.

Then she threw up on the floor of the booth, but the policeman had already gone.

"It happened by chance. I never knew how the investigation got started."

"And why did she come back and report the strippers? The damage was already done."

"She said it wasn't right, she was sorry for you and Aurelio. She doesn't seem very smart. Maybe she's envious because the others didn't include her in the scam; perhaps before, she was afraid they would find out it was her and have her beaten up. It makes sense to me, she said the others kept company with the worst clients. We're making inquiries but the dancers have closed their bank accounts and gone away. I'll keep Aurelio posted."

"It all seems so complicated. Why didn't the strippers ask Mario and Aurelio for the money directly instead of getting other people involved?" she asks the policeman.

"Would you have taken them seriously?"

Caterina shakes her head.

"What will you do now?" she asks, squeezing her hands between her thighs.

If the stripper hadn't informed on them the nightclub would still be operating now. She and the policeman would never have got to know each other, Aurelio would not have learned how to make hand shadows.

Caterina would like to telephone the dancer who caused her apparent ruin, or go by her house, but she knows she won't find her there any more.

"I've asked to be transferred to an office job, if they agree I think I'll start an evening degree course," says the policeman.

"Like old people who resume their studies after retiring?" jokes Caterina, showing her dimple, and he gives her a nudge in the ribs with his elbow, then scratches at a spot of paint in the palm of his hand. She gives him a questioning look.

"I gave my mother a hand with some work on the house," the policeman explains, focusing his gaze on the magnolia-coloured walls of the room on which the paint lay thick and cement-like.

"This is where we fucked the first time. But the room's different."

"Don't be vulgar," Caterina chides, punching him on the leg without looking him in the face, then when she catches his expression in the mirror it takes her breath away.

"Have you fallen in love?" she asks, laughing, and he grimaces.

"Perhaps."

"Aurelio and me. It's something that goes way beyond anything else. You can't even call it love. It's something that has always.... *existed*," says Caterina, but the policeman puts his hand over her mouth to silence her.

He used to do it all the time, especially at the beginning, when she tried to tell him how she was feeling; with him she could cry or shout only during an orgasm. When Caterina asked him why he couldn't talk or express certain feelings he replied, "There's no point in hurting yourself."

At first she thought it was a cruel and distant thing to say, then she understood.

The policeman gets up from the bed and goes and stands by the windowsill, resting his shoulder against the chalky wall, which leaves marks on his shirt.

"The walls were pink. And from the window you could see a stall selling food, all priced at nine euros ninety-nine cents, with photos of kebabs and sushi. I remember thinking I wanted to go and get some even if I died of food poisoning," he tells Caterina.

"And there was a half broken-down fan in the corner," he goes on, making expansive gestures in the manner of a surveyor describing the room. "It wasn't even necessary because outside it had just been raining and there was the smell of the storm. And the bathroom was on this side, not that side," he says, going in there to check what colour the towels are and whether there is any soap. "That time there wasn't any soap, I remember, so I didn't wash my hands properly. Then I went home and realised I still smelt of you," says the policeman, his voice muted by the half-open door to the bathroom.

Caterina starts crying, biting her lips, so that he doesn't hear her sobbing, but he comes back into the bedroom and sits beside her.

"We can't go on seeing each other," she tells him, with her

fingers pressed to her eyes.

"I know."

Caterina breathes in slowly, her body still shaken by the odd sobbing spasm.

He takes her hand and strokes her palm with one finger.

"You once told me that drug addicts aren't ugly when they're taking drugs. You said they get ugly only when they stop or reduce their doses; that's when they break out in spots, lose their teeth, get a runny nose and become scary. But when they're on drugs they're radiant and vibrant like lovers," he says to Caterina.

"I remember… you said you wouldn't know about that because you'd never touched drugs in your life," she says.

"But now I know what it's like," he says, squeezing her hand and pressing her knuckles. He is almost hurting her but Caterina gives a return squeeze. "I feel more scruffy, more lacklustre. At the beginning I never had to check my phone to see if you'd written something, you were always there. I never had to go looking for you or reply to you because I knew I'd be able to find you if I wanted to. It was a great feeling. It calmed me. It made me wake up happy even when we didn't speak or didn't see each other."

"Well, for me it was dreadful. I was always nervous. You made my blood rush," says Caterina staring at the floor.

"Whereas now I know you might not answer if I call, and that you don't need that call. When I came into the hotel lobby you looked at me the way you did the first time I came into your boyfriend's nightclub and you didn't yet know who I was."

"That's not true, you can't go back in time. I'll never be

able to look at you like that again."

"But you do," says the policeman, making her lie back and pinning her arms above her head with one hand. Caterina holds her breath but the policeman does not kiss her; he feels her breast and her stomach with his free hand, then strokes her thighs and stops only when she closes her eyes.

"You don't feel anything. You're going back to the point where I don't exist any more," he says, releasing his grip, breathing heavily.

They lie there for a while, then Caterina murmurs, "I'm sorry."

The policeman does not reply, she gets off the bed and gathers up the sheets heaped on the floor. She straightens them out, then starts to fold them.

The policeman puts his jacket back on; Caterina opens the cupboard and lays the white cotton sheets on top of a blanket.

"You know that theory that says if you save my life then I will always be indebted to you?" says Caterina.

"Yes, they put it in a load of films. But it's not theory, it's just common sense. Everyone feels grateful to whoever has got them out of trouble," replies the policeman, and she is pleased to see him smile.

"I think it's not you who is indebted to whoever saves you but the person that saves you who wants to keep giving you something, for ever. It's the person that saves you who is unable to move on."

"Take care of yourself," says the policeman shaking his head, and Caterina opens the door to go back down to the reception.

The place is still empty and the note she wrote saying she

CLEOPATRA GOES TO PRISON

would be back soon has fallen to the ground. Caterina picks it up and puts it in her pocket, then she hugs the policeman and watches him as he walks out of the door. His body is already a shadow.

14

"That idiot woman who spoke to the police – I can't believe it," says Aurelio, banging his head against the wall.

Before coming to see me at the hotel, the policeman telephoned Aurelio to fill him in on the latest developments. When Aurelio turned up at my apartment an hour ago I pretended not to know anything. I took his soaking wet fleece off him and I towel-dried his hair while the wind rattled the windowpanes. He stroked my stomach and then we rubbed noses without kissing, biting each other's ears and nuzzling each other.

However, after he had told me the whole story, I overplayed how let down I felt by some of the dancers I had thought of as friends, but he was too agitated to take any notice of my reaction.

"Perhaps she wanted to spite Mario. He was clearly going behind her back," he says pacing backwards and forwards in the sitting room, and I try to make him understand that despair or love is not a girl's only motivation.

Aurelio goes into the kitchen and starts getting things out of the cupboard – even though he doesn't live here he's bought almost everything.

"They've disappeared. Mario, those bitches, all of them," he says while he decides which saucepans to use. Outside it has stopped raining and through the open window I glimpse iridescent puddles; the wind has an ammonia-like smell.

I start setting the table, then I say to him: "I hope the dancers at least manage to pay for some cosmetic work on their breasts and buttocks," and Aurelio gives me a hurt look.

"I don't understand why you're so obsessed with cosmetic surgery," he bursts out, the way he does when he sees some actress on television disfigured by botox.

He doesn't know, doesn't understand, that some women do it to start over again with a new body rather than to avoid aging: it's not a second chance, or a bid for eternal youth – that artificial life is for many women their first life.

The extortion racket organised by the strippers is the least sad story I can imagine. I'm angry but unlike Aurelio I don't hope they get HIV from the first guy that turns up on a tropical beach. I don't like it when he talks like that and sometimes his bitterness puts me off – but I'm not the one that ended up in Rebibbia.

"Let's change the subject," says Aurelio when we sit down to eat.

I start drinking the wine then I get up to fetch a photo my mother brought over having found it in a drawer. Her house has turned into an archaeological dig but unlike me my mother is not afraid of toxic finds, and the vapours of memories don't poison her.

"You were so skinny and odd," says Aurelio, examining the photo in which I have my hands raised jokingly in a sign of victory because the examiner had just told me I'd passed my driving test.

He took that photo himself, before inviting me to get in his car and drive round and round the car park, hooting the horn, the way they do in wedding processions.

"I remember the day I saw you outside the school. You looked sullen and stiff-backed, and you wouldn't look anyone in the face," he says laying the photo on the table and continuing to eat.

I finish drinking, then tell him I've lied to him.

Aurelio puts down his fork and twists his mouth.

"I was right," he says without taking his eyes off my face. "Don't tell me anything, I don't want to know. I was in prison, you could do whatever you wanted," he insists, then gets up to fetch a cigarette from the packet lying on the windowsill. In the evening twilight the pillars on the worksites that are still operating look like a forest of iron, and in certain places the lights on the cranes give the sky a faded pink glow. But perhaps that's just an effect of the storm.

"Sit down," I say, trying to calm him.

"I don't want to know about it now," he replies, going to fetch his jacket, his body too cumbersome for him to know what to do with it.

"You remember that time we went to the circus?" I ask and only at that point does Aurelio collapse onto the sofa.

I move nearer without getting too close, careful not to annoy him with any display of affection.

"You remember when we saw the snakes?"

He nods, still confused.

"There was a fortune-teller who wanted to predict our future but she only read the tarot cards for me. Afterwards you asked me what she'd seen, and I told you that she said I was special, but that wasn't true. You know what she actually said to me?"

"Wine always goes to your head, and it's getting worse," says Aurelio, and even though he is smiling I know he is still quivering with worry.

Aurelio is forced to live in a constant state of foreboding: before Rebibbia there was not this sense of danger but now we have to live with it. Now we have special sensors, we are like tame canaries sent into coal mines to detect pockets of gas and to die before everyone else. Now there is something in Aurelio, something in me, that makes us hypersensitive to catastrophe but although we can interpret the signs it doesn't necessarily mean that we'll be able to escape in time or to warn others and save them.

Maybe we have always been like this, and increasing hardship instead of leaving us crippled has made us privileged, easily taken advantage of but also special, destined to be aware of the lowest and most obscure levels of society and to make them known even when we cannot do anything to improve them.

"She said that one day I will leave Rome, I will have three sons by two different men, I will cut my hair and not let it grow long any more, and about the age of forty I will die of breast cancer," I tell him all in one breath, surprised I can remember everything in the same order that red-haired girl passed sentence on my future.

"Well, at least you have another nine years to live," he says shaking his head.

I give him a punch on the upper arm and hurt myself. Since he has been doing regular workouts again his muscles have gone back to being that compact nervous mass my body is used to.

"I don't understand black magic. What's the use of tarot cards if you have no hope of a better life."

At night Caterina stretches out on her mattress, which is still lying on the floor, and although she does not have any particular dreams she feels a diffuse warmth rippling through her body and behind her eyelids she senses the silver and lilac undulation of the stars, heavenly bodies expanding and dissolving to blend with the light of the street lamps that punctuate the road on which she lives, a road that unfurls in a tangled skein of bypasses and slip roads until it leaves behind the city in which she grew up, a brick-filled pit of quicksands fortified by habit and by a future that never arrives, where the river catches fire at sunset and the sun that strikes the apartment buildings and spills over them transforms Rome into the place she will never leave, a crevasse in which Caterina sinks and breathes with her eyes closed, all tarmac and wretchedness, until her muscles gently push her back up again and she returns to a sweet and edgy destiny, toned by workouts and by love; the city where she gets up every morning even before the alarm clock rings, and walks between the bushes through the knee-high grass in the park, beneath the noisy comings and goings of the birds, until she reaches the bus stop – a mystery person, with her

CLEOPATRA GOES TO PRISON

elegant, lop-sided gait, still told by passers-by that she walks like a dancer.

Dedalus Celebrating Women's Literature 2018–2028

In 2018 Dedalus began celebrating the centenary of women getting the vote in the UK with a programme of women's fiction. In 1918, Parliament passed an act granting the vote to women over the age of 30 who were householders, the wives of householders, occupiers of property with an annual rent of £5 or graduates of British universities. About 8.4 million women gained the vote. It was a big step forward but it was not until the Equal Franchise Act of 1928 that women over 21 were able to vote and women finally achieved the same voting rights as men. This act increased the number of women eligible to vote to 15 million. Dedalus' aim is to publish 6 titles each year, most of which will be translations from other European languages, for the next 10 years as we commemorate this important milestone.

Titles published so far:

The Prepper Room by Karen Duve
Take Six: Six Portuguese Women Writers edited by Margaret Jull Costa
Slav Sisters: The Dedalus Book of Russian Women's Literature edited by Natasha Perova
Baltic Belles: The Dedalus Book of Estonian Women's Literature edited by Elle-Mari Talivee
The Madwoman of Serrano by Dina Salústio
Cleopatra goes to Prison by Claudia Durastanti

Forthcoming titles include:

Baltic Belles: The Dedalus Book of Latvian Women's Literature edited by Eva Eglaja
The Price of Dreams by Margherita Giacobino
Venice Noir by Isabella Panfido
The Girl from the Sea and other Stories by Sophia de Mello Breyner Andresen
Fair Trade Heroin by Rachael McGill
Primordial Soup by Christine Leunens
The Medusa Child by Sylvie Germain

For further information please contact Dedalus at
info@dedalusbooks.com

Dedalus would like to thank the individuals and organisations who helped fund the translation of *Cleopatra goes to Prison* via kickstarter. Their names appear below in alphabetical order:

1. Jack Allen
2. Graham Anderson
3. R Anderson
4. Debbie Auld
5. Roderick Beaton
6. Antonietta Beck
7. Eva Bosch
8. Peter Bush
9. Maurice Caldera
10. Central Books
11. Michael Coffey at Peribo Distribution
12. Creative Fund Backerkit
13. Andrew Crumey
14. Margaret Jull Costa
15. Dickon Edwards
16. Geoffrey Elborn
17. Isabelle Fredborg
18. Dennis Forsgren
19. Pat Gray
20. James Guerin
21. Daniel Hahn
22. David Hebblethwaite
23. Marina Sofia Ionescu
24. Katrina

25 Brendan King
26 Xavier Leret
27 Kirsten Lodge
28 Mark
29 Alex Martin
30 Deirdre McMahon
31 Alistair McGowan
32 Gary Miller
33 James Morrison
34 Muireann Maguire
35 Ania Ready
36 Oliver Ready
37 Marisa Ready
38 SCB Distribution
39 Eoghan Smith
40 Geoffrey Smith
41 Alan Teder
42 Turnaround Publisher Services